DARK TALES – VOLUME 3

Edited by Dorothy Davies

DARK TALES – VOLUME 3

GRAVESTONE PRESS

TABLE OF CONTENTS

It's A Long Way Down (Rie Sheridan Rose)

The river banks were deserted—not even one of the gang to be found. Billy Peterson looked longingly at the cool green water flowing under the bridge. It was ninety degrees in the shade and he felt gritty with sweat. Swimming alone wasn't smart—but it was sure tempting. He heaved a sigh of disappointment and turned back toward the house. At least he could switch on the fan in his room and take a nap. Better than baking his brains.

Just as he started away from the river, he heard a voice call his name... so softly he thought at first he was hearing things.

'"Who's there?" he called back.

'"Come swim with me, Billy," the voice wheedled.

'"Is that you, Sarah?"

'There was no answer to the question, but the voice went on. "Take your shoes off and come in... the water is heavenly."

'Billy kicked off his sneakers and socks and skinned out of his jeans, glad he'd thought to wear his suit under them "just in case." He pulled his t-shirt over his head then had a brief qualm.

'*What the hell am I doing? I should at least make sure it's Sarah before I jump in...*

He dropped his shirt beside the rest of his clothes.

What does it matter? Some girl wants to swim with me. Does it matter who she is?

He dove into the water. It felt like hitting a tub of ice after the steamy heat of the summer day. He broke the surface sputtering and searched for the girl. A brief second thought flashed through his mind—and then a head popped up in the center of the river.

The girl was beautiful, ethereal. She made him forget all about Sarah. Hair the color of moonlight clung to her skull in sleek waves. Even at this distance, her eyes were definitely as green as the river, though he knew that should be impossible to see.

She lifted from the water enough for him to see that she wasn't wearing a top. Her skin was ivory in the sunlight, the tops of her breasts just clearing the water.

He licked his lips involuntarily. *Damn, she's hot. I've never seen her before—someone that smoking hot I'd remember.*

He didn't care about the cold any more. A few sure strokes took him to her side. He grinned at her, treading water.

"Well, here I am. What's your name, sweetheart?"

She cocked her head with a coy little smile. "My name is Ondine."

"What's that, French?"

She shrugged.

"Not that it matters. It's pretty. You're pretty. Damn pretty."

She giggled a little, raising her arms from the water and twining them about his neck. "Why, thank you, sir…"

He grinned at her like a lovesick puppy. His arms encircled her waist. "Whaddya say we get out of the water and go somewhere a bit more… comfortable?"

His legs were tiring. Treading water was hard work. Quite a lot of exercise when you weren't used to much more strenuous than twiddling your thumbs on a video game.

She shook her head. "Why don't we go to my place?" she whispered.

"Anything you say, little lady."

She leaned forward and planted her lips on his. The kiss was cold and somehow a bit—slimy. But it was a kiss and he hadn't had a whole lot of experience. Maybe it was normal.

He tightened his arms around her slim waist, closed his eyes and deepened the kiss. His lips parted and her tongue insinuated itself into his mouth.

It was a cold, clammy worm, reaching way further down his throat than a tongue should be able to go. His eyes flew open.

The girl—thing—in his arms was no longer beautiful. If anything, it looked like a giant mutated fish of some kind.

He made a strangled sound deep in his throat and tried to pull away from her.

The arms around his neck were deceptively delicate—and covered now with iridescent scales that scratched at his bare skin. The tongue—or whatever it was—in his throat probed deeper and he gagged.

She began to submerge, taking him with her.

He panicked, struggling to free himself, but she was just too strong. The water closed over his head, spilling into his half-open mouth. He fought harder, but to no avail.

Down, down, down. To the bottom of the river.

He had no more breath. He had to…

… and the water filled his lungs.

She slid her tongue out of his mouth. "It's a long way down," she whispered. "Welcome to my home."

And she propped him up with the others.

Dizzy, but no Wormhole (Geoff Nelder)

Memory is a fickle thing. I believe I am awake yet before my eyes work my nostrils were invaded by the smart tang of iodine. No. Disinfectant but not pine, nor sandalwood, nothing that I recall.

With gradual awareness of pain everywhere from big toes—yes they wriggle—to my skull, and my ears assaulted by a non-remembered electronic whining I force reluctant eyelids to open.

It's a hospital room. It must be for this is not my room, or bed. Too narrow, too clean yet what hospital would use green sheets? It clashes with the pink walls. A clinic then, specialising in some weird ailment I must be suspected of having. But how?

I was out cycling this morning, to the shops to buy…what was it? It'll come to me. I can't have dementia at only forty-one, surely. Ah yes. To Starbucks in Euston to meet with…what's her name? I'll go through the alphabet; that always works. Alice, Ann, Belle, Bonnie, Bryn, Carrie, Claire. That's it! Lovely auburn-haired Claire with plaits down to her waist, last time we met to discuss marketing my invention. She's brilliant at promo and my simple gadget to self-peel lemons needs all the help I can get now that I couldn't get past the auditions for Dragons' Den.

Did I suffer a bicycle accident? Temporary trauma amnesia then. My fingers and toes all move, so do my knees though my neck is stiff and sore. I raise the nauseatingly green sheet to peep at my body, which is in a yellow gown. It's like a Peppa Pig cartoon in here. Definitely not NHS but I have no private health insurance. Maybe the driver's rich and is paying for this. The gown has no fastening round the front so all I see is my normal hairy legs and pink toes and sun-tanned hands. A mirror for my face please. I could use my phone to see my face and call Claire to find out if I need to apologise for being late, but there's no locker or cupboard beside me to explore for my mobile. Nor button to summon help.

"Help!!"

A yellow door had been hiding in the yellow wall but now opens letting in a red-faced woman dressed in khaki dungarees.

"No need to scream this place up and down, Buzz."

Strange sentence. "Sorry. No, my name is Derek Brown. Why am I here and where is here?"

"Don't be more stupid. Derek isn't any kind of a name and Brown? Who on this planet would have a colour for a name? Buzz Sawyer is it you are from blood tags."

"Buzz Sawyer? Isn't that the name of a WWE wrestler? It's not me!"

She tidies my sheets and aims what looks like a taser at my forehead. "Maybe possible she said it

12

was Buzz. Lie still. Thirty-seven, ninety-eight and sixteen over twenty-one. You'll live."

"DNA should identify me. I had a genetic test."

"Blood tags use DNA. Calm stay."

Strange speech mannerism. Maybe she's a Romanian nurse. I try again. "Wait please, nurse. Who brought me in and where am I?"

"No nurse I. Decider; that's who I am."

I don't like the sound of that. "If I'm all right, can I leave now?"

"Stay till fetched. We is in Crenton of course."

"I'm unfamiliar with that name. Is it in London?"

"What Lundun is? Everyone knows who passes the tests, that Crenton is capital of England."

A map. "I've a map on my phone if you give it back to me. Or do you have an atlas?"

She doesn't seem to possess a mobile phone but rummages in a locker drawer and pulls out a crumpled paper and hands it over. "Where you from?"

It is of the British Isles. There's the Isle of Wight, Scotland, Wales but in England where London should be is a dot labelled Crenton. It's on the River Times. There's a random knitting pattern of roads with no recognisable motorway names. Of course, my mind has created this nonsense in this dream I'm inhabiting.

This is madness. Just a moment, am I in a mental institution and instead of being a nurse, this woman was one of the inmates? Apparently not; she wore a name badge. 'Dec. Mel Stone'. There's that

13

Dec for decider again. Decide what? My life or death?

I try with a more conciliatory tone. "Excuse me, Decider, why am I here?"

"Found, unconscious in the road. Recents Park near."

She must mean Regent's Park—that's near Euston Station. "Did I have a bicycle accident?"

"Bicycle? What is?"

"Oh, come on. A bicycle. You know. Two wheels and two pedals you use with your feet and a saddle to sit on." I was losing my tone rather rapidly.

She chortled. "Really? You have dreams so strange."

Of course. This must be all a dream, or nightmare. I push back the greens to get out of bed. Although I ache all over—probably from a real accident on a real bike—I am well enough to walk and wake up properly.

"No, no Buzz, you were lost to consciousness, a concussion. Observations so stay."

"Listen, Deciding Stone, this…" I wave my arms around. "…is all a dream and I want to return to reality. My previous life."

She laughs at me as if I'd just fallen out of a Christmas cracker as the joke. '

Saliva drools out of her unhygienic mouth. "How do know you that your previous life—as call it you—wasn't a dream because I know I real am?"

Absurd. I rub my forehead as if that helps. "I am forty-one years old. I have that many years of memory as a child, my sisters and parents, school, university and my career as owner of an engineering firm making helicopter parts. I know dreams travel at the speed of light in our heads but not forty-one-years-worth of living in one night!"

"Well, buzzy-bee, it seems like did you. What be a hell copper?"

Not again. Either she's a fantastic leg-puller or this is *the* dream I need to wake from. I need to get out to speak to other people, see outside, find a bloody bicycle. I attempt once more to get up but suddenly she pulls back her arm, swings it around and slaps my face, Hard. I can't believe a nurse would…and I did nothing to stop it.

"What the hell are you doing? That's assault!" My hand is on my heat-throbbing cheek as I fell back onto the bed in shock.

"Buzzboy can't leave. I bring restraints?"

"What? No! I insist on discharging myself."

"Not possible. I summon Super Ordinator."

"This is a hospital. Right? With care for patients running short."

She stood, hands on hips ready to smack me again. "As you engineer be, no. Again you dream. Reality you be an indentured servant. That's why you cannot leave without master."

"A slave? Now I know you're joking. Where's this Superman you've summoned?"

The yellow door reopened to allow in a stout man. Shock of white hair yet he looked to be in his forties. Like me. His khaki uniform was like Decider-patient-beater but with a scarlet broad sash running diagonally from his right shoulder to his waist. I have no illusions of getting more sense from him.

He coughed. "Lumpen Buzzz Sawyer. Your master nearly here. Transport you then to his auberge. Be well."

He turns to leave, so I shout, "Wait. I have a family. A wife! Well ex-wife but—"

Another slap from decider sends me speechless onto my back.

"Indeed. Your allocated wife be there. You have been hers for a decade. Be well or be dead."

I want to ask him more but the death threat and another slap from Nightmare Nurse shuts me up. I need to think.

How can I show that this is not my real life?

I pinch my arm, hard. Damn that hurts and it makes Decider frown at me as if she's the only one allowed to inflict pain.

"May I see my medical notes please?"

"Forbidden."

"No, I have the right under the Data Protection Act to see information about myself." I leave out the exception relating to mental instability.

"Forbidden. No such law."

I scrutinise her in an effort to detect a lie, lots of lies. Black hair, sky-blue eyes, normally attractive in both genders. Hers go deep, nearly transparent. But yes, I see a devilishly twisted demon. Damn, it's my reflection in her eyes.

I sink back into and between the lumps in the mattress and deeper in despair. Must be a dream. If

I go to sleep I'll wake up back in England. My England with a real London, bicycles and no slavery except for unfortunate illegal immigrants.

I'm afraid to go to sleep. Suppose I 'wake'— assuming I am awake now—in a worse scenario: bottom of a deep well; tied to a railway track; being chased by a fast-running, hungry alligator; or in a mad hospital ward where I'm turned into a slave for ever breaking rocks? For any of those, the thing is to escape.

I pretend to fall asleep. A while later all is quiet so I risk opening one eye a smidgen. No sign of Oberführer Decider so I slip out of my lettuce-coloured sheets and tiptoed to tall lockers for clothes more appropriate for outdoorsy non-patients. Something non-yellow please. Damn, a choice of one—pink. Ugh. Fine if when I get outside everybody is wearing pink, but suppose they'll all in black, but me?

I rummage in the other lockers. No clothing, but boxes of needles, gloves, instruments like weird pliers that look as if they should be in a garage rather than a hospital. Nothing labelled NHS. Most have a green logo of an infinity symbol and the words: Value First. The kind of label on cheap tack. I tuck scissors and tape in the coverall pocket, roll it up and creep open the door. No one in the yellow corridor. Same colour as the floor and ceiling too; everyone would look jaundiced. The next ward, room, cell, whatever is empty but a large window draws me like a magnet.

At least the sky is blue with white cottonwool balls, and the horizon has the appearance of London with similar skyscrapers, steeples, cranes and tower-blocks. Now to see what's below. Is the grass green? Ah, I'm five floors too high to jump, and yes there are pink people scurrying about their business.

I search the room for more clothes but have to slip on the pink overall over my yellow hospital gown. Yes, there's a map on the wall. It's the British Isles in shape but none of the names make sense. London really is Crenton and other cities have changed names. More, Bristol is a forest, Birmingham is a huge lake and Oban is the largest city. Crazy. A paper on the nurse's desk has a picture of me. Buzz Sawyer. She'd not made it up, someone else did. No! A smaller picture of my allocated wife, Brenda Sawyer. Spitting image of my vicious ex—Aileen, who'd spit in my tea, burn me with her funny cigarettes, bring drunk men home. A cold shiver runs up me. I screw up the paper and throw it away.

No one in the corridor. I choose the stairs rather than a potential trap lift. On the first floor I look for another room to search for money, shoes, anything useful. More pink clothing but the only footwear is a pair of loose-fitting khaki surgical boots. They'll do. No wallets or purses in pockets or drawers.

Back in the corridor too late to avoid two khaki-clads strolling towards me. I look askance but they're too mutually-engrossed to notice me. One was followed by a perfume cloud. Unidentifiable but a pleasant hint of roses widen my nostrils. I walk my mismatched boots to a foyer. A horseshoe reception desk is busy with two people with heads down looking at something. I assume computers but see no screens as I know them. I head for glass doors but hesitate. Is there an identity feature to access them? A fingerprint button, retina scope, or simple push? I wait until someone comes off the paving and pushes the door and nip out before it closes.

That's it. I'm out, in this nightmare.

It's London almost as I know it. Distinctive yellow-brown brick terraces and iron railings but hardly any traffic. No yellow lines on the road. I risked looking up. No cameras, unless they're vastly different in this world. Nor many people, perhaps it's now Sunday. I see a group walking towards me so I dodge behind a large London plane tree with its familiar peeling bark. I fondle it hoping to ground myself in Nature. The men and women wore pink or orange coveralls, so I wasn't out of place. Another wafting of fragrance lingered in their wake like a comet tail. Freesia.

I have the urge to do two things: go find this allocated wife though not to be captured into slavery, and to locate my accident spot. Maybe it's a cusp in time and space and I can return. Decider said, or meant, Regent's Park. If this is a dream it's the strangest one I've had and lasting so long, especially when I'm trying to wake up so many times.

I creep close to the walls, shop windows selling not-quite familiar clothes and wares until I realise

19

how suspicious I might look. At least nearly everyone are in various shades of pink. Do civilians have an enforceable uniform? Some wear red stripes down arms and trousers and it occurs to me they might be slaves. I walk down the middle of the pavements but with averted face although that too must look odd. The street layout of Crenton is not dissimilar to that of London with additional and subtractional alleyways and sculptures. Strange to see so many bees everywhere. I soon find the equivalent of Regent's Park, which indeed has the wrought iron, gilded Jubilee gates but with the wrong date.

I used to cycle through the park as a short cut even though I was shouted at and so now walk my usual route looking for signs of my accident. Some places have scratches on the tarmac or cobblestones. Am I looking for blood stains? I don't know how much blood I lost to the blow on my head and push up my sleeves looking for recent wounds. None. About to give up the search I spot something peeping out from under a rhododendron bush with its shiny dak-green leaves.

It might be my black rear pannier bag! My pulse throbs faster than a jack-hammer in my neck. That would be brilliant if so since it might still have my phone and they'd not robbed me of it in hospital. As if it would work in this nightmarish parallel world. I bend to grab it but freeze and straighten up. Suppose it's somehow attached to my 'other' existence. Would I be crushed in a wormhole, die, or be stunned and find myself back in a hospital run by weirdos?

I find a stick and poke it. Nothing happens. If I touch it with my khaki surgical boot will I be insulated from any effect? I emit a short laugh then look around in case anyone has seen me. I'm a fool. I want an effect from the only memorabilia from my own London. I should touch it with my skin. I nearly do so but hesitate. Fear of a violent death shoots perspiration from my face and shakes my fingers. I must do it, so I stretch my right hand then change to my left in case it shrivels. I should preserve the one I do everything with! A few millimetres to go. I grab for the handle on the canvas bag. Before my hand reaches it my whole body convulses, throwing me backwards, falling flat on the path. Winded. I look around and see pink-clothed people in the distance. Damn. Dizzy, but no wormhole.

A bee zigzags towards me and persists in bothering in spite of me batting away at it. Then the penny drops with a clunk. The droning is because it's a drone. As all the other insect-like eyes in the sky. No CCTV because this lot have perfected miniature, energy efficient spying machines, unless…unless they really are bees repurposed to serve human controllers. Either way, I'm in their scope.

I hear heavy probably-khaki boots behind me just as I launch myself at my cycle pannier. This time with mega-determination for skin on canvas.

"No, you don't, Buzz Sawyer."

I'm thrown sideways by a burly woman hurling herself feet first into my body. As my vision reddens with rage, pain and frustration I just see a hint of twisted bicycle wheel further under the bush.

"My name is Derek Brown. A free man."

Shrieks of laughter from several of the bastards, one of whom apply plastic ties to my wrists.

"This is a dream. Let me wake up, please!"

A man in khaki with a black beret, gold studs on his epaulets and stinking of garlic says, "Who talk to, Sawyer?"

"Derek Brown!"

Smack on the back of my head.

"Lies. You're Buzz Sawyer, lowly Lumpen, servant. Nothing to save you now. We burn off one of your feet and send you back to your wife and master."

He turns to the rugby tackler. "Good work, Brigand Smyth. If he'd reached that contraband artefact we would have lost him to the otherworld."

Still in a daze that last statement fills me with a smidgen of hope. They know there's another existence. I bide my time.

***

An hour or so later I'm in a different room. No bed. No chair. Just a hole in the floor but too small for me to climb down. The numpties hadn't found my scissors so I cut the plastic ties and wait behind the door.

Footsteps and a muffled humming. I'll have to chance it on only one guard entering. When the door opens inwards I throw myself at it. A woman guard bangs her head against the doorjamb and falls in. I haul her in and peep out in the corridor. No one. I drag her further in away from the door and tape up her wrists, ankles and mouth. Red hair. Nice. I have a penchant for... I ignore the food tray. Might be drugged.

I still have my pink coverall on so I sneak out.

I hide until dark before creeping to Regents Park. Yes, no. No my bag's gone, yes, the bike is still under the laurel bush.

Ten minutes later I'm riding north down dark, quiet alleys. My bike's protesting with an annoying squeak but hopefully only I can hear it. I hurtle down a steep cobbled lane that threatens to dislodge all my teeth but there's no houses, just industrial units. Damn, I emerge onto what I know as Church Street. Lots of houses, people, drunks, police... I slow and aim for shadows. Luckily its night, but most won't see me anyway 'cos I have no lights!

I'm aiming for a house on Church Street North where an aunt used to live but should be empty. I'll break in and after a few weeks lying low I'll figure out what to do. No—

I didn't see a row of black dustbins. Damn not having lights. I'm not hurt but the noise! I'm on my back wrestling with the bike and kicking off a bin when laughter reaches me.

"One too many, eh?"

"Playing ten pin blowing with himself as the bowl!"

"Is it a woman or a bloke? Is that pink?"

Hands roughly pulls me up by my armpits and a torch blinds me. I slump with defeat. Thoughts of how they're going to burn off my foot sends paroxysms of nerves up my spine and perspiration leaking from every pore.

"Hey! I know who this is. You thought you'd get away, didn't you? Missing since Tuesday, said on the news. What's your name B something…"

I slump even more in resignation and mutter, "Buzz S—"

I screw my eyes up in the torchlight.

"Brown, that's it, Derek Brown. Weren't you abducted by a UFO in Regent's Park, mate?"

They all guffawed, patted me on my pink-coveralled back and took me for a compulsory pint at the Hole in the Hedge pub.

Of course. I'd connected or reconnected by touching my bicycle. I'm never going near Regent's Park again.

A pint of Old Man's Spit later my vision blurred. No. Was this another dream?

I Pull my Blanket up Tight Beneath my Chin (SJ Townend)

Mumma says *if you stay in your bed all night, no walkies, no tears, I'll take you shopping at the weekend.* Says she'll buy me the doll with the eyes that blink when you rock it. Not only does the doll blink, but when you lift the little trapdoor on its back and pour water in, it fills its nappy. And it cries so you can wipe away its tears. I really want that doll. I don't think I can do it though. The doll will never be mine, because night time is when the fingers comes.

At story time, I clamp onto Mumma. She tells me not to be *silly* when I ask if I can keep the little light on. *Big girls don't sleep with the lights on*, she says and she swipes on her phone with its shining screen while I super slowly continue to turn the pages of my third picture book.

Mumma keeps her phone by her bed. It glows all night long, tells her the numbers of the time so she knows when to get me up for school. I see it when I stand by her in the night.

She reads the words *The End* but Mumma isn't looking at the book, she's swiping on her phone but I don't mind as long as she's here next to me, in my bed.

One more story? Please Mumma, one more? I beg.

She says *No. You've had three. Mumma needs alone-time.* Why would anyone want 'alone time'? *You need sleep now, Sweetpea. School in the morning. Won't learn anything if you're tired. Sleep tight.* And that's when I pull my blanket up under my chin and Mumma pushes the sheets in extra snug, pretends to wrap me up like a birthday present. The fingers aren't here yet, on the wall, but I know they'll come.

Mumma slides away and my bed feels like a boat and the dark, dark floor which licks against its sides is the ocean and I can't see the bottom of the sea but I know there's something swimming down there. *Night-night, Sweetpea. Mumma loves her little angel* she says and pulls the door to as she leaves.

Mumma, I cry, *leave it open,* so she pushes it open a little for me and I think about what she said: aren't 'little angels' just good dead people?

Mumma says *you can have it 'ajar' Little Pea, but no lights. Light is not conducive for sleep. You need it dark to rest, Angel Cheeks.* And I've no idea what she means but my door is open so I say *'thank you'* and *'love you'* and think for a moment about whether it's just my cheeks that remind her of dead good people.

Mumma switches out the big light and leaves again. I'm in total darkness, eyes closed *or* open. *Mumma please, come back. Draw the curtains tighter* I say because that's how the shadows get in. Because I can still hear her on the landing, walking away, so I know she can still hear me. She comes

26

back in, pushes my curtains together in the middle where the gap was that lets the fingers in. Then she leaves again. *Love you,* she says again, *love you for infinity* and I don't know what 'infinity' means but she says it all the time because her Mumma says it to her. Think it means forever.

The fading creak of footsteps lets me know she's not lingering like she sometimes does to check I stay in my bed. She's definitely left, gone downstairs. I hear the door to the living room squeak open. The low buzz of the television set hums on. If I keep stock-still, I can hear the faint melody of the starting music of her favourite show. It's a comfort—of sorts—but I know it's only a matter of time before I see it at the foot of my bed.

Wind outside whistles in through the vent by my window and—*whoof*—the curtain moves.

Dull orange light from the street lamp illuminates a patch on the far wall of my room. Looks like a tiny, dim, screen. There are no pictures on my wall. Mumma says I mustn't decorate the room. Something about keeping it smart for the landlord.

The sight of the orange patch makes me fill my lungs up with air and rock from side to side to pin the sheets that cover me down with the sides of my thighs. Body. Must. Stay. Underneath. Got to keep myself covered up from the *other* blanket, the one that smothers, which is the blackness of the night.

I shift back as quietly as I can, I prop my head up slightly against the wall behind me without letting the blanket slip off. As I scoot back, that is when it happens. I freeze. The shadow fingers appear on the wall.

Mumma says *it's the tree outside*. The tree the landlord keeps saying he'll trim back but never does. Mumma can't reach it herself, too high. But it's not a tree. I know exactly what it is. It's a witchery finger. It creeps along my wall and as the wind blows and shakes outside, the long sharp claw moves closer. Something's arm stretches along and around and soon it'll reach the corner-bend and travel along the other wall all the way until it reaches me in my bed.

I want to stretch out my own arm and reach for the bedside light and flick the switch but that would mean the dark would touch my skin and if the dark touches my skin, then the bad finger can too. I keep the blanket tucked in tight under my legs, my chest, my arms and the cheeks of my bottom by pressing against it from underneath down the sides of my thighs and around and under my toes. I want to call out, *Mumma, help me*, but if I speak, it will hear, the thing outside my window—

And I know it'll reach me first.

Over the tapping of the claw on the window, I hear a thumping in my chest and the burr of the muffled television noise downstairs where I know Mumma is. I think about the doll: its big smile, flicking eyelids, the little trapdoor in its back. Want that doll. But right now, I want Mumma more.

The television noise and the promise of Mumma feel further and further away and the end wall of my bedroom with the shadows is looming closer and closer.

I rip out of bed and run like the wind, without looking behind me, not even once. Down the landing, zoom. Stumble down the stairs. Push open the door of the living room.

Mumma's favourite armchair—I see it. At the top of it, I see her soft, brown, curly hair. Sometimes she smells like vanilla ice-cream. I creep over, knowing full well she'll send me straight back to my room. Always does. If I walk slowly, maybe she won't notice me. I'll curl up next to her chair and stay there, forever, by her side.

Her cheeks are pink, tight balls pushed up underneath happy eyes. I see all of her teeth as she throws her head back with laughter. At least she's watching something funny. Last week, I came down late and caught her watching something full of blood and nightmares and *dink dink dink*. A bad man called Freddie. Is he the one who's been tapping at my window, *dink dink dink?* Mumma didn't know I watched her watching it—I'd stood so stiff and quiet for so long behind her comfy chair.

Now, she is *really* laughing, like a donkey. She snorts too, when she sees me. The loudness of her laughter scares me more, makes me cry. Why is Mumma laughing when I'm so scared? Why does she find my unhappiness so funny? But she is still my Mumma and I know she'll make me feel better, safer, so I run up to Mumma. She wipes the tears from my face.

Oh Sweetpea, she says, *did you have a bad dream? Mumma's here.* Her face changes. She's no longer laughing but looking at me with a face that says she wishes I wasn't in the living room but also a face that is her face, Mumma's face. It's a face which cares for me. She picks me up onto her lap and I tell her I haven't had a bad dream, haven't been to sleep yet. Can't sleep. The monster by my window is back, tapping on the glass, stretching out its claws again.

Mumma hugs me in tight to her soft chest. I feel her hair against my cheek. Feels scratchy, not soft like you think it would from afar. Smells of spicy dinners. She tells me *everything will be okay* and *it must've been a dream because there are no such things as monsters* and she'll always protect me because she loves me so much. *I love you so much, Sweetpea,* she says and I ask her *how much?* and she says *so, so much* and I ask her does she love me enough to let me sleep in her bed and she laughs and says she loves me *to the moon and back,* she'll love me *for infinity* but she needs her rest and I'm *too fidgety.* I reach out to touch the dark bags under Mumma's eyes she points too and I know she is tired but not as tired as me.

Please don't make me go back in my bed I beg but Mumma is 'staying strong' and carrying me up the stairs, walking with me in her arms along the dark, dark landing.

You must stay in your bed, Sweetness, my Darling Angel, she says and she draws the curtains together tight.

30

I pull the blanket up and under my chin, squeeze my teeth together until they grate and think really hard about her not leaving the room. If I think hard enough about her sliding into bed next to me and making me safe with her arms, maybe she'll do just that?

Can I sleep in with you? I ask. I already know the answer.

Darling, no. We both need a good night's sleep, she says. She kisses me on my forehead. It feels wet and cold and the black dark makes it feel like an ice kiss. *I've work in the morning and you've school. Get some rest. Love you infinitely,* she says and goes.

I say, *please,* one more time, *can I have the light on*? Mumma's voice changes, deepens. She says *No,* a firm sound. I know not to ask again. *Go. To. Sleep.* She says, in the deep, firm voice and walks away too quickly because she wants to ignore me or perhaps she doesn't hear as I ask her to *please push the door open a little more, so I can still see light from the landing.*

Blackness.

I lie there forever and ever and stare at where I know the wall at the end of the bed is until I can sort of make it out. My eyelids feel heavy. I think I close them for a count of three. But then a gust of wind outside pushes the curtains open. The orange light and the bony finger are once more cast against the far wall. I bite down on my lip. My fists are tight balls screwed full of bed-sheets. I can't hear the mumble of the television. I hear nothing except wind and tap-tapping of fingers on glass. I want to scream. I don't. I can hold it in. Must hold it in. But if the long claw which seems to be growing, stretching around the corner of the room reaches me, I know I'll have to scream. Might be the only thing saves me. My scream. But then, a scream'll draw its attention, make it see me, lying here huddled up, my sheets tucked in tight around me. I swallow the scream down. If the finger touches me, everything's over. It'll take me with it, outside, through the glass of the rattling window and I'll never see Mumma again. Never. Forever. And forever is a long time.

Mumma feels a million miles away. I feel scared, like the time we found our cat sleeping the long sleep at the side of the road. I also feel angry. I also feel a bit okay because I know Mumma loves me *to infinity* and she'd never leave me in danger, so maybe she is right? There are no such things as monsters.

Need to be a big girl. *Big girls aren't afraid of the dark.* I'll think about the doll. Think. About. The. Doll. If I get it, if I stay here in bed, I can be its Mumma, rock it when it cries, comfort it, look after it like Mumma looks after me.

Then I hear the tapping again at the window. Panic floods. I can feel I'm still in it, but it is as if my bed-boat has capsized, I'm tumbling into the ocean, I'm only small, can't swim yet, can't touch the bottom. I hold in my scream, but nearly wet the bed.

32

There's no orange glow from the landing light through the slim gap between my door and the wall. Mumma must've turned it off; must've come upstairs; must be in her bed. I can't hear the television. I know she'll be cross, but I can't lie here and face the creature. Its finger is stretching further. Closer.

I slip out, swing open the door and charge along the hallway. It's pitch black and never-ending, like an underground tunnel. I have to get past the top of the stairs, but on the wall at the top of the stairs, there's *another* patch of orange light with creeping creature fingers shaking up and down in time with the wind and with the snores I think Mumma is making all in time with the thumping in my chest. I walk as fast as I can without running— because I don't want to trip and go down the stairs, and because running is noisy. Don't want it to hear me.

Somehow I make it to the other side of the house where Mumma's room is. By her bed, I see the light of her phone displaying the numbers which tell her the time. The white-blue glow tells me Mumma must be there, in the bed, as does the bumpy outline of her body I can see covered up by and tight underneath her quilt. As I get closer, creeping now, don't want to wake her, I know I must slide in next to her so she can guard me while she sleeps. I hear her snoring. It's louder than the banging in my chest.

33

Wish she was awake and it was day time and we were down in the kitchen, making pancakes, painting pictures. What if she never wakes up and I'm left alone here in the dark forever or until the creature at the window hears me scream because I'm sure I'm going to scream eventually. Don't think I can hold it back much longer. Mumma lets out a loud snore. Makes me jump. How can she protect me if she's asleep? In the darkness, I scull around the bed, closer to the phone light, to the side where Mumma's face is. If I can see her face, know she's really there, everything will be better.

I find her sleeping face. Mumma snores again. The bottom of her mouth falls open, then closes. I stand still in the darkness, by the side of her bed, comforted by her resting face. She sounds like an animal when she breathes in her sleep, but she's Mumma. I love her *infinity* even if she makes odd noises. It's cold. I want to be under the safety of her covers. How can I get in next to her without waking her up? Without the monster with the boy's claws hearing me?

One chance.

I get one go at this, because if she wakes, I'll be back in my own bed, alone, facing a sort of certain death.

I slide my hand under the duvet in front of Mumma's chest. There's just enough space for me to get in between her and the edge of the bed. The phone light shines on her face, makes the edges of her hair glow too. For a heartbeat, she looks stiff and still, like a dead person. A cold angel.

Mumma snores again. I pull my hand back from the bed-sheets quick-sharp because her eyelids flicker a bit when she sucks in air through her nose, as the sound of the snore honks out. *Mumma, please don't wake up!*

Something runs over my toe. A spider, a hand, a skeleton's finger. A hand from under Mumma's bed. I can't see and I don't want to see what it was. Can't help it. Scream comes out. I jump onto the edge of Mumma's bed. Mumma's arm flaps up. She makes the loudest snore and with it, her jaw snaps down too far.

Crunch.

Her head rolls back off the pillow. Her eyes flip open. I see by the light of her phone her green eyes aren't green anymore and they're pointing in opposite directions. The middles—where it should be green—now glow blue-white, like an ice angel, a death angel. The phone light dims. Her eyes dull, become scratched brown buttons. I scream again but even though her eyes are open, they're dark bottomless pits, and she isn't waking up.

Another noise comes out of her mouth but this time it's not a snore, it's louder than a snore, it's a long, sharp, *screech*. Fork on a plate. I ram my fingers in my ears. It's not her voice. She's talking in a sharp language I don't understand. Don't think I want to understand. Feels like if I understand, Mumma will be gone for good. It's too high and scratchy to be her voice. I feel wee run down my leg.

35

Ripples travel up her bent-back-too-far throat. Out from the pit black darkness of her split open mouth comes a bony claw. It pushes out further and snaps off her teeth, one-by-one, until her face is nothing but blood and red and gum.

Snap.

Crunch.

I scream but can't look away.

The claw keeps coming and coming and coming, out towards me, forever and ever. I can't stop screaming. There is nowhere I can go and my chest is exposed, all bar the thin cotton nightie I have on and Mumma is awake but not. Her head snaps right back. I shimmy back until I'm on the edge of the end of the bed. I can't move anywhere else. It's coming. The claw extends and I'm trapped and it taps me on the chest and keeps pushing forwards, against me, harder and harder. I screw my eyes closed, try to ignore the pressure on my chest and squeeze my balled fists as tight as I can and I scream and scream and scream.

***

I wake up in Mumma's bed feeling terrible, worse than when I had flu. It's morning. Daylight blazes through her bedroom window but she's not here and the claw's not here. I remember everything up until the finger tapped me on the chest.

I pulled the sheets around me. I tuck them tight under my chin. I hear Mumma speaking with her normal voice. She's on the phone downstairs. I make out some parts of what she is saying: *unhinged* and *no sleep* and *I'll take her in late then. You're right, best to keep a routine.* I realize she's talking to Gramma because Mumma ends the call by saying, *love you infinity, Ma.* And then Mumma comes up the stairs. I want to see her but I also want to be as far away from her as I can ever be.

When she comes into her bedroom, sees me sat pressed up to the headboard with the sheet all tucked in around me like an Egyptian mummy, she asks how I'm feeling.

I say nothing. She looks normal. But it can't be her. She sits by me, strokes my hair, tells me all the normal things she tells me in the morning: I'm her *favourite Angel Face* and *would you like eggs or branflakes?* and *we're a little late but we should make it in before break.*

My tummy turns over a full curl. Need away. Fast. Gramma lives miles away, I'd never find my way there, but maybe I'll feel safer at school.

I get dressed, eat hardly anything, then she takes me to school. She lets me sit in the front seat of the car. Every time we stop at lights she looks over and asks *you okay, Sweetpea?* And then she answers her own question, *sure, you're fine. You're a big girl.* I look at her eyes. They're not ice angel eyes, they're her normal green eyes. And her head is where it should be, how it should be. Normal green eyes and normal curly brown hair and a mouth full of normal looking teeth and her breath smells bitter and a bit bad which means she's drunk some coffee. Is it all okay now?

Love you lots, Sweetness. Love you infinity, she says as she kisses me goodbye. I shudder as her lips press wet, cold on my forehead. *Sleep in bed with me tonight, Little Pea. No more bad dreams.'* I grab my satchel and back out of the car. She blows another kiss and drives away from the school gates.

***

I make it in just in time for maths. I'm tired. We huddle around on the rainbow rug and the teacher asks us all to count in tens. Everyone stops when we reach one hundred; everyone except for the kid to my left, this brainbox. He keeps on going. The teacher encourages him, *well done. How far can you go?* And the kid keeps going for what seems like forever. He stumbles when he gets to two hundred and ninety and this other kid—even smarter than the first—chips in, says she can go all the way to *infinity.* The teacher asks her what *infinity* means and this kid says it means when something goes on forever and ever and ever, never ends. I feel myself yawning because I'm so tired and I don't recognize any of these strangers around me and then I close my eyes for a second and then I feel something tap me on my chest. I scream so loudly, all the other kids scream too. Then I wet my pants. Mumma comes to pick me up, but when she comes, I refuse to go home with her.

***

I'm seventeen now, maybe eighteen. The priest with the melted face and the glove of blades who visited last said *you've been speaking Enochian, child.* Scratchy, high-pitched always leaves my throat red raw. *You speak the language of dark angels.* Wouldn't tell me what I'd said during my last seizure. Feel like if I did know though, if he ever did tell me what my tongue had forced out through my lips and teeth, I might lose myself completely.

Did I ever fall back asleep? Maybe I never woke up, that night when Mumma's head split open and the infinite claw tapped me on the chest. Perhaps I never escaped, I'm still asleep.

I sleep rarely now, only when the medication kicks i, and when I do, I find myself back in my childhood bedroom, with sheets tucked under my chin, waiting for the curtain to twitch. I'll dream the same dream, again and again, night after night— always Mumma in bed, her cranked neck, smashed teeth, lit by the light of her phone and always the claw, extending forever from her sliced wide maw, an infinite telescope, probing only for me in the darkness. At times, the dream feels more real than any waking moment and there are times I know it's just a dream. There are times when I think the moments I spend awake are in fact the dream and the dream is in fact what is real. Each night, I lie alone in this small room as the handful of brightly coloured tablets kick in. I drift, hear the gust of wind, the sound of gentle snoring. If I let my lids fall, I see Mumma. Not the Mumma who comes to

39

visit me monthly out of a sense of duty—morose, silent, distant and grey now that she is—but the Mumma who I loved and trusted. Once. I hear the crunch of her neck snap back, see the infinite kaleidoscope of shadow-bones ratchet out from her mouth. I run. I run in my sleep even though thick, leather cuffs tie me to the bed in the here and now, because if I stop running, it'll tap me on the chest and I will scream. My neck is cold, my sheets have slipped.

I wish I could pull my blanket up tight beneath my chin.

Nobodies (Stephen Lang)

I'd never seen a dead body before. Apart from my Nan, that is, but she didn't count. The undertakers did a great job with Nan. Dad and I kissed her when we said goodbye. She felt stone cold when I brushed my lips across her forehead, but she looked nicely made up, comfortable and too cosy to be a proper dead body. So, no, Nan didn't count.

Ugly dead counted. Unclaimed and laid out like rotting meat for the flies. The morning I woke up on a mortuary slab, I lay between a man and a woman. I knew they were corpses because of the smell. You could almost taste the fumes. They'd been scrubbed clean with bleach.

The three of us all wore matching white smocks. No buttons, just a pullover one-piece. Comfortable enough for nightwear if that's your thing. Not my sort of pyjama party.

My foot tickled when I stood up to get a better look at my white-smocked companions. I couldn't undo the tight knot of string. No matter how much I contorted, I couldn't get close enough to see what it said on the label.

Dad would say that was me all over. Blind as a bat. Too vain to wear glasses. Too disorganised for contact lenses. But my eyesight wasn't that bad and besides, how often do you need to bend down to read a label attached to your toe?

The sensible thing would have been to get out of there, but I was curious.

Strands of greasy black hair half-covered a hole in the man's forehead the size of a pound coin. But there was no blood, as the wound had long bled itself dry. He had the beginnings of grey stubble on his face. I wondered if hair kept on growing after death.

Like me, he had a label tied to his toe. Then I got it. I'd seen such a setup in forensic crime dramas on TV. A crude means to provide identification.

Name: Michael Beckett
Hair: Black
Eyes: Blue
Height: 5' 9"
Weight: 75kg

It didn't tell me much. The eyes, well, they were both shut and I wanted to leave them like that. Height and weight? Would that be accurate? Didn't dead bodies shrink or contract in some way?

I still couldn't bend or twist enough to read the label tied to my toe. I wasn't as fit as I'd kidded myself to believe. I made a mental note to ask for a refund for the Pilates classes.

The woman had a bloated face like she'd puffed out her cheeks and the wind had changed to keep them like that. There were dirty marks around her neck. I thought the cleaning wasn't as thorough as I'd first assumed until I saw they were black bruises.

I couldn't see a label attached to her because I couldn't see any feet. Maybe she was too short for the smock, but I didn't want to lift it to investigate further.

Then I saw it tied to her thumb. The thumb stuck out crookedly like she was hitching a ride. *Get me out of here.*

Name: Mary Beckett
Hair: Auburn
Eyes: Hazel
Height: 4' 10"
Weight: 65kg

Husband and wife. The labels had at least told me something.

I'd broken a nail trying to undo that stupid piece of string. What would mine say?

Name: Joanna Simpson. Joanna. Don't call me Jo.

Hair: Brown, with dimensional highlights. I'm thinking of going full brunette again soon.

Eyes: Green. Dad always said he was so proud of giving me my green eyes. Although a boy at school with colour blindness once swore they were blue. He called his condition tritanomaly. *Anomaly.* I liked that. That he was different and it might rub off on me. Simon - yeah, that was his name - he

43

gazed into my eyes for so long I almost agreed with him that they were blue.

Height: 5' 4". No, more like 5' 6". Say 5' 7" in heels.

Weight: Mind your own business.

I didn't know these people. I didn't care about them or their dismal deaths. It was time to get out of there.

I couldn't see a mirror. Only a metal sink with two taps and a small table covered with medical instruments. Forceps, scalpels and scissors. One of those electric carving knives. The room had a single door, which I assumed was the way out. Not even a toilet in there.

The door clicked open. I lay back down on the slab. I felt guilty, like getting up and walking around had somehow broken the rules.

A man in a white coat came in. He looked like a doctor or medical examiner. A uniformed police constable followed behind. They didn't speak, focused on whatever they were there to do.

They spent a long time preparing. They washed their hands in the sink and put on gloves, masks and plastic hair coverings that looked like shower caps. The police constable stood head bowed, waiting for the other to take the lead.

"Shall we?" said the medical examiner.

He turned Michael Beckett's head to the side to show the police constable a hole at the back the size of a tea saucer. It wasn't as clean as the wound at the front, a mess of bone, blood and hair. The medical examiner raised his eyebrows, clearly pleased with his big reveal.

"Point of exit. He shot himself in the head after strangling his wife."

I couldn't see much of the police constable's face behind the mask, but I knew the colour had drained from it.

"Sounds so - so - cold-blooded."

He took a side step and walked into the table covered in medical instruments. He almost had it over. The medical examiner took his arm to steady him.

"Are you alright?"

The police constable put his head in his hands. I thought he was going to throw up. But it wasn't that. He was crying.

"I know them," he said. "The Becketts. They lived next door to my parents."

The medical examiner placed his hand on his shoulder.

"Oh my God, I'm so sorry. It must be a shock for you. This shouldn't have happened."

I sensed kindness in his voice. I wondered why he had chosen this calling in life.

"It doesn't matter," said the police constable. "I knew them a long time ago. I always thought it was too much for him. But this?"

"Maybe you ought to get off?"

"No, I'm fine. There's still stuff here to do."

They were preparing to turn their attention to me, so I closed my eyes.

The medical examiner pulled up my right eyelid. He had the gentlest of touches.

"Green eyes," he said. "Still bright in death, but soon they'll begin to spoil. Such a shame. Such a waste. A pretty girl. Is it wrong to say that in the circumstances?"

The police constable took his turn to lean over me. He pulled up my left eyelid. It was a long time before he spoke.

"No," he said. "Not green eyes. They're blue."

"Blue?"

"Yes. Her eyes are a beautiful blue."

The voice was familiar in its decisiveness. It took me a moment to recognise it.

"Simon?"

He turned to face the medical examiner and pulled off his mask. Yes, it was Simon. He hadn't changed much. He looked like a boy in a grown-up's uniform.

"Why is she positioned like this between Mr and Mrs Beckett? There isn't a connection, is there?"

The medical examiner shook his head.

"No. Nothing in it at all. Nothing poetic or sinister to worry about. The mortician should have taken more trouble to show a little - sensitivity. But there are so many of them to get through, you know."

Mr and Mrs Beckett. That was what Simon always called them and it all came back to me. Beckett was such a vain man. He dyed his hair that

46

horrible jet black, greasing it back from the top of his forehead. Simon didn't like it when I called the man Dracula, but he made the perfect vampire with that black widow's peak. Mrs Beckett was just as bad in the hair department. I always thought her auburn bun was a wig because it was so perfectly coiffured. But it seemed it was real enough. I guess those labels don't lie.

Mrs Beckett was disabled, although people used crueller words back then. It was fear. That was all it was, partly because nobody could put their finger on what was actually wrong with her. Sometimes she was in a wheelchair, other times she hobbled around using two walking sticks. I'd also seen Mr Beckett carry her from his car into the house. His hair fell forward and he cursed her as he shook his head from side to side to keep it out of his eyes.

Simon took my hand and looked at my nails. I wondered if he knew the colour was called Bordeaux. Could he see the shade of deep red? Did he see orange instead or brown? At least they hadn't tried to bleach me clean.

"What happened to her?"

"Suspected overdose," said the medical examiner.

He pulled up my smock and pressed the tip of a scalpel against my bare belly. But I knew he wouldn't hurt me because of that kindness in him. He looked into my eyes. And I was right. He hesitated and dropped the scalpel. Right on the floor like he never wanted to touch one ever again.

"No," he said. "I don't need to inflict further harm. Suicide will be my conclusion."

Simon turned over the label that was still attached to my big toe.

"Oh. No name?"

He didn't remember me. Otherwise, he would have filled in the blanks. Joanna. Not Jo.

"She hasn't yet been identified," said the medical examiner. "It happens a lot. Nobodies. Makes it all the more tragic. I worry that their souls can never settle if we don't find out their names. Do you think that's fanciful of me?"

Simon didn't answer. He wouldn't understand about being fanciful. He was intensely focused, even when he was sixteen. That was the problem. The only thing that really made him different. He wanted to start the sixth form with a clean slates and there was no room in his life for me. He still found time to run errands for those irritating neighbours, though. A vampire and his dependent wife, how could he? Deep down, I knew it should have been me who ended it. It should have been my call. I tried to shrug it off, but I broke down in front of Dad. He was pretty calm about it.

"You're young, Joanna," he said. "Things will get better. You can do better." I'm not sure if I ever did.

"So," said the medical examiner. "That's why I always say *not yet*. There's a chance we'll find out soon who she was. Hopefully, someone will come forward. It's possible. Likely, even."

"Nobodies?"

48

"There's a hell of a lot of them."

"Yeah," said Simon. "Tragic."

***

I thought they would keep coming back to see me. To see how I was doing. I hoped there might even be a spark of memory from Simon. But they never came back.

Not yet. At least the medical examiner tried to be optimistic. *Likely, even.* I'm sure these things take time. Dad will be here soon to say goodbye. Dad won't let me down. I know I look good lying here. Comfortable. Cosy, even. Nothing at all like a dead body. Just like Nan.

49

Watching You Without Me (Paul Edwards)

Wind screamed, thunder rolled, rain blinded my eyes. I zipped my coat up, then sprinted across the car park into the Cheese and Grain. I stood sheltering from the storm in the bustling reception area, eyes glued to the window.

Outside, merchants and traders bundled produce into black bin sacks, dismantled stalls and lifted iron poles into the backs of vans. I listened to the hubbub of the indoor market – people buying, selling, haggling. I smelt slabs of meat sizzling on grills, French cheeses and an assortment of exotic herbs and foreign spices.

Someone tugged at my sleeve. I turned to see a pretty young woman with jade-green eyes smiling at me.

She blushed. "Oh," she said. "You don't recognise me."

"Should I?"

She put a hand over her mouth. "God," she said, "sorry! I thought you were somebody else."

She turned away and I awkwardly stood there watching the rain stream down the windowpane. Then, after a pause, she turned again and said, "You're a Capricorn."

I narrowed my eyes. "Do I *know* you?" She shook her head. "I mean, you thought I was…"

"My mistake. You look nothing like him. Up close, I mean."

"Who did you think I was?"

"A friend."

She glanced outside. "Looks like the rain's beginning to ease." She took a deep breath. "I'm Anja. I'm a Gemini. Listen, do you fancy grabbing a coffee?"

She must have seen the look on my face, because she added: "No big deal. Just, I haven't got a lot on and I could do with the company." She smiled again and I knew there was no way I was going to say no.

We sat in *Cordero Lounge* on stools beneath a print of van Gogh's *The Starry Night*. It turned out Anja lived in Frome. She owned a top-floor flat above a popular Aromatherapy shop. She was in her second year of an Open University degree in Psychology and was hoping to become an educational psychologist by the end of it.

"I'm fascinated by people," she said. "By behaviour, mainly. I want to know how we work. What makes us tick, you know?" She flicked her hair away from her eyes. "What do you do?"

"I'm an IS engineer. I travel around a lot, fixing computers, installing software, that kind of thing."

She nodded. "You enjoy it?"

"Not really. Sometimes I feel like I'm in this rut, you know? Driving out to the same old places, fixing the same computers..."

She laughed. "The moon enters Capricorn on Friday so the time is ripe for change. The full moon at the end of the month signifies an emotional high tide. It's the best time to make changes, you know."

"You really believe in that stuff?"

"I'm *intrigued*, I guess. Over the years I've studied astrology, cosmology, palmistry…"

"You read palms?"

"Occasionally," she replied.

"Think you could read mine?" I stuck my hand out. "I've always wanted my palm read."

She leaned over the table and I caught the scent of her perfume. It smelt oddly familiar somehow. She took hold of my hand and said, "You have two brothers and one sister. Your father passed away just over a year ago."

I stared at her. "You got that from looking at my palm?"

She nodded and smiled.

That smile was bewitching.

We went back to her flat. It was small, much like my own. The single window in the sitting room had the most astonishing view over Frome. She'd replaced all the doors with bead curtains, strung up fairy lights and painted the walls a dark, lurid crimson.

"What's that?" I asked, pointing to a strange prickly plant and a blackened crystal on a fold-out table.

"Some of my occult stuff," she said.

We sat together on her sofa and talked for ages. She said all the right things, seemed to know so much about me. Later, after sharing a bottle of wine, we made love in her bed. In the darkness she moaned and writhed, her fingers splayed out across my chest, her green eyes shining.

That night I had this disturbing dream. I was alone in Anja's flat. On the mantelpiece, candle flames fluttered like tongues. I drifted toward the mirror and there, hanging in the darkness, was my own blood-red reflection. My image quickly faded and then Anja appeared, green eyes burning, her hands shooting out and shattering glass, pulling me through the frame into a dark abyss.

***

"Don't go," she said as I dressed for work the next morning.

"What do you mean 'don't go?'" I searched amongst our clothes on the carpet for my jacket. "I *have* to go."

She stretched herself out across the bed. "Stay. Phone in sick or something."

I stared at her.

She stared right back with those cold bright eyes.

I said, "Why don't we go out tonight? My treat. I'll take you to that Italian on Vicarage Street."

"Sounds nice," she said as I pulled my car keys out of my pocket. "But why can't we stay here? Just you and me, Chris. Wouldn't it be great if we never had to leave this flat again?"

She sat up, wrapping her arms around herself. "Sorry," she whispered. "I know some of the things

53

I say are strange. I get carried away, that's all. I don't know why I just said that, about never leaving the flat." She sighed and hung her head. "You must think me weird."

"No," I said, shrugging into my jacket, but her glassy stare remained fixed to the duvet and she said nothing more.

***

It was a week later. Anya and I had arranged to meet at my place for seven. I left work early and was back in Frome by six. Rain scratched at discs of light around streetlamps. I grabbed some groceries in the Co-Op and a cheap bottle of Pinot Noir. Then, just as I was leaving, I saw Helen standing under the awning outside Iceland.

Helen's a work colleague. She's tall and thin and has long brown hair and a bright, pretty smile. "What are you doing here?" I asked, crossing the road to meet her. "Thought you'd moved to Wells!"

"I did," she said, smoothing her hair out of her eyes, "but my mother lives in Frome. I was off today so I thought I'd do some shopping for her."

I told her about what had gone on at work today and about the team meeting we'd scheduled for Monday. "Fancy grabbing a coffee?" I said.

"Sure," she replied. "Why not?"

We took a table in *Cordero Lounge*. We talked work for a while, then about life in general.

"Feels like my life's gone off on one," I said as I stared into my coffee. "I had all these set goals and plans. I wanted to be married by the time I was thirty. Have kids and everything." I looked up, gazing at the swirling brushstrokes in the van Gogh print on the wall. "Is that sad?"

She shook her head. "No, not sad. It'll happen, Chris." She chewed her lip. "You seeing anyone at the moment?"

"Yeah. Well, kind of. It's a bit… strange, to be honest."

"Strange?"

I laughed. "Yeah. The things she knows about me. There's definitely a spark, a connection, but it sort of feels contrived. I don't know how to explain it…"

She traced her finger around the rim of her coffee mug. "Is this the person you spoke about before?"

I shook my head, momentarily confused. "I don't think so."

"Me and my bloke, Tom," she said, "have been on and off for years. It's just, we get ideals in our head, don't we? Of how relationships should be. Perhaps we should just face up to the fact that we can never find the perfect person. It's an impossible…"

She stopped midsentence. Her eyes locked on something outside. I turned quickly. "What?" I said, looking through the window.

The street was deserted.

"There was a woman out there just now," she said, "staring in at us."

"Where did she go?"

"Not sure."

"Listen," I said, reaching for my wallet, "I'd better go." I smiled. "I really enjoyed our chat."

"Me too." Helen grinned. "We'll have to do it again some time."

I hurried home, oblivious to the low rumbles of thunder coming from above. Rain tore through trees, created hypnotic patterns in puddles. I turned down the narrow lane at the back of the garages and saw Anja in the communal garden outside the flats.

"Anja?"

We stood staring at each other for a moment. Then she lowered her eyes and said, "Are you going to let me in or what?"

I let her in, then closed the door behind us. Anja perched herself on the foot of the bed. "What's the matter?" I asked.

"Who was that girl you were talking to?"

"Girl?" You know, the brunette. I saw you in the café together."

"So?" I stared incredulously at her. "Her name's Helen. We work together; she's in town visiting her mum. Look, what's this about?"

"What were you talking about?"

I ignored her and walked off into the kitchen. Opened a bottle of wine and poured myself a glass. I heard her feet pad into the room and then turned, trying to keep the disgust from my face.

"The first time we met," she said. "In the Cheese and Grain. Then, later, in the café. What would you have liked to have heard? How could I *really* have impressed you?"

I didn't respond, alarm bells ringing inside my head.

She drew a hand across her eyes. "I've fucked up again, haven't I." Her voice trembled. "I can't help how I am. I mean, nobody could love you like I do. And watching you without me... Well, it's wrong. Wrong for both of us, Chris."

I stared at her. "We've only known each other for a week."

She hung her head so I couldn't see her face and she laughed bitterly at the floor. "Next time," she said. "Next time I *promise* I'll get it right."

I had another lucid dream that night. Anja was leaning over me, whispering words I just didn't understand. I smelt something burning deep inside the room. She straightened up as I tried to focus on her voice, to hear her words, an enigmatic smile creeping across her face.

"Don't hate me," she said. "It's a chance to start afresh. The onus is on me, right? To make it good. To get it *perfect*."

I stared at the blackened crystal in her hand. She touched me on the face with trembling fingers and then there... *is*... a flash, and I... I don't remember... I don't remember anything else.

I look around, confused. Dawn light steals through the curtains. I'm disorientated, feel vaguely nauseated. I can't even remember what day of the week it is. I fling back the duvet and pull on some clothes, drifting over to the gilt-framed mirror by the door. My face stares back, so pale and blank looking.

Outside, dead leaves swirl across pavements. I slip in and out of shops in a daze. Clouds stack over trees and chimney pots. Then a sudden downpour streaks my face and I zip my coat up and dash for shelter in the Cheese and Grain.

Inside I listen to the rain chatter on slate tiles, slosh through broken guttering, whisper against grimy windows. I hear the bustle of the indoor market, watch the rain outside make hypnotic circles in wide, dark puddles.

Someone tugs at my sleeve.

I turn and see a face that is, for a split-second, strikingly familiar.

The young woman retracts her hand. "Sorry," she says, putting that hand over her mouth. "My mistake." Then she takes her hand away again and says, softly, "I thought you were somebody else."

Ghastly Ties (Olivia Arieti)

"They're back," whispered the keeper's wife, "Sir Francis and Lady Cecily are in their room."

Joe gazed at her, "What nonsense, Nellie! The dead can't come back and you know it."

The owners of HollowPike mansion had died years ago; the horrible tragedy hit the whole village and the locals still shuddered with grief whenever they passed by the deserted structure.

The couple was spending the afternoon by the nearby lake with their son, Vincent. Despite the weather not being too good and the ripples turned into waves, they jumped into the water. Shortly afterwards they began gasping and, by the time the boy ran in, his parents had already disappeared; sadly, the powerful vortices dragged him into the deadly depth as well. The following day, their bodies were stranded on the shore, swollen and blue, inexplicably, one next to the other.

Sir Stuart Ronsell, a distant relative and the only inheritor, promised to return after the funeral and settle the issues regarding the sale of the property.

Now and then Nellie entered and removed dust and cobwebs, while Joe took care of the garden.

Years passed, but the new owner never showed up.

On her deathbed, Nellie assured her husband once again, "they flashed by when I was tidying up.

Lady Cecily kept staring at me, her eyes full of tears," and added, "they rank among the undead now…"

When Joe stopped looking after the garden, the house quickly assumed the aspect of a decayed and abandoned one and a sinister halo hovered above it. Nettles and weeds carpeted the paths, uncouth shrubs replaced the flowerbeds and the ivy climbed thickly upon the panes and doors.

Early one morning, he too distinguished three shadows in the garden and that same night, bangs and thuds resounded from the upper chambers while the shutters opened and shut; tremulous lights filtered through the curtains and the old man was so bewildered that he ran in to check what was going on.

"It's great seeing you again, Joe," said Francis and clapped his shoulder with his clammy hand.

"I'm so pleased we have the chance to let you know how much we've appreciated your devotion," smiled Cecily, whose drooping jaws chilled his blood.

"Vincent will be overjoyed, too; he has gone down to the lake, seems he can't resist the call," said his father.

So strong was the agitation and terror that the poor fellow dashed out, fell down and hit his head; he died on the spot.

"We had to come back," said Cecily to her husband. "We owed it to Vincent."

"What if we hurt him more?"

"You can't condemn our boy to the everlasting tenebre without ever being in love... After all, we are the reason of his death."

"I fear what might happen if he does fall in love... We are no longer as we were, darling, you have to accept that."

The house was inhabited again, but it looked as grim and lugubrious as a family burial chapel.

At night time, crows and ravens perched on the turrets, bats glided around and mournful wails resounded from the massive walls.

The locals noted the strange animation and all agreed the house was haunted.

More than once they swore they'd spotted Vincent walking along the village streets or at the inn.

His parents were often detected by the lake where the ripples danced mercilessly before them as though whispering, "You should have known better, guys, lakes can be very treacherous."

That's when Cecily would start crying and huddle in her husband's arms.

Regret and feelings of guilt for their carelessness were overwhelming and they would have done anything to give Vincent his life back.

When Mauve, the late Sir Ronsell's daughter, arrived with the intention to finally sell HollowPike, the locals hurriedly informed her about the dreary presences.

Although the young lady considered the scary rumours mere nonsense, she resolved to lodge at the inn as the house was too big and the keepers dead.

Her stay provided the chance to visit the village and linger by the lake.

"So you like it here too." A warm voice reached her from the back.

She turned round abruptly; a handsome young man was smiling at her.

"I didn't mean to frighten you, Miss."

"No, no, it's alright."

"It's my favourite spot, taking a swim is what I like most, no matter the season."

Mauve kept staring at the newcomer.

"Too bad you can't join me."

Before she could reply, the guy was already swimming away and rapidly faded in the distance.

That evening, she was surprised to find him at the inn.

"I hoped to meet you again," he said and invited her to his table.

Mauve accepted happily; she, too, liked the brawny fellow.

When she told him the reason for her stay, Vincent's face darkened. "My parents and I are momentarily dwelling there," and sighed. "We'll be very sorry to leave."

The girl wasn't aware of the presence of tenants.

"Please come and visit us, my folks will be delighted to meet you," he said and took her hand.

Despite it being rather bony, a pleasant warmth pervaded her.

Then he hurriedly got up and disappeared before reaching the door.

The following morning, on opening her room's window, Mauve wondered if the area was doomed to an eternal mist. The grey veil that fell upon the houses, lanes and trees was as gloomy as unnerving.

Right after breakfast, she headed towards HollowPike, anxious to see Vincent again.

Her excitement couldn't be concealed, just like the unrequitedness that took hold of her whenever she thought of him.

The door was ajar, the corridor long and dark. She made her way to the living room where Vincent stood, looking out of the window.

He turned round, "I feared you wouldn't come."

The tone was apprehensive, the glance frightened.

"No reason I shouldn't," she smiled, "have to get acquainted with my property."

he place was cold, candles were flickering here and there like melancholic souls and the fireplace looked as out of work for ages; the clocks weren't working either, their hands immobile on the midnight hour, the mirrors had turned opaque and everything seemed to have never been moved, just like in an enchanted castle under an evil spell.

Perhaps, it was a haunted house after all.

"My parents are down at the lake, but they'll be back soon."

"Are those your folks?" she asked, hinting at the picture on the mantelpiece.

Vincent nodded, "It was love at first sight for them," and unexpectedly took her in his arms, "just like mine for you."

Then he kissed her with the ardour and despair of a last kiss and held her so tight as though he'd never let her go.

And unexpectedly, she, too, was consumed by his passion, felt her heart melt and would have remained in his arms forever.

"I… I don't know however I'll manage without you, honey," he muttered.

Vincent's attitude was perplexing. His glance, words and acts had something final about them as when a lover is on the point of pronouncing his ultimate adieu.

"Why do you have to leave?" she asked.

The young man lowered his eyes just as two presences, enwrapped in dripping shrouds, entered.

The hair was sticky, the limbs muddy and the faces swollen.

"Our time's up, my dear," replied his father's spectre.

Mauve gazed at them, petrified.

"Don't be afraid," said Cecily in a hollow voice. "We simply wanted our boy to fall in love, just like it happened to us. We couldn't forgive ourselves for being the cause of his…"

"No, Mom, no, say no more," pleaded Vincent. He stood before his beloved like a zombie, scraps of flesh hanging from his limbs and the head a frightful skull.

The elder spirits hastily pulled him away and all vanished in the darkness.

Never a more heartrending cry filled the air.

Mauve was so terrified that she slumped onto the sofa and fell into a swoon.

The sun had finally re-established its domain when Mauve woke up, but the unusual brightness wasn't enough to sooth her anguish.

What looked like a nightmare was a true romance, even if a ghastly one.

Vincent's presence flashed before her; he was waiting for her and she knew exactly where.

"Hey, I'm ready for that swim now," she cried.

"Don't you think it's a bit too cold, sweetie?"

"As long as I'm with you, I'll be fine," and she stretched out her hand.

Nobody ever knew what happened to Mauve and her body was never found.

Fear and distress increased among the locals for the couples' spirits were often seen swimming in the lake or roaming along the shore as though unable to abandon the scenario of their dreadful demise.

Corners of the Room (Rickey Rivers Jr.)

A four sided prison, a singular room, the landscape pale, folded; I reside. Here I have been ever since. Since when do matters of fact mean anything to unbelievers? I arrived in my prison weeks ago. I arrived supposedly babbling. I am told my tales of the tongue are fictitious. I know my tales are true. In fact, they aren't even my tales. They are the spoken truths which lie in corners of the mind. The corner of a physical room can trap all manners of mould and mildew, of web of sight unseen. I've seen the corners of every room since chanting the sacred incantation, an incantation once unfamiliar to my lips. I was influenced to repeat the words as they came to me in dream. From the third eye one can see valleys. And my eye of plenty revealed itself valleys of impossibilities.

In dream came words on tongue and in the waking world came the eye, the eye in the corner of the room, which began in my bedroom, has followed me all the way to where I currently reside, this four sided room, this geometric play pen, no playthings but imagination and dream itself. And dream itself can haunt and prod. A dream can even be reality. All that matters is point of view.

My view started at home. At home I was simple, a happy man. I went to work. I paid bills. I ate. I slept. I was all together decent and all together ripe, ripe for the pickings of creatures from another land.

The common misconception of alien abductions is the belief that an extra-terrestrial being would simply extract a subject from their residing planet and take them elsewhere. In my case the extraction was simply mental, a transportation to another place, another time, with beings who were building length and building wide, all with different colored exoskeletons. These were the beings of dream, a reality from a different view. And the view of me from my bedroom was taken from the eye in the corner, no doubt surveillance from visitors who would only interrupt mentally, yet refusing a physical intrusion.

I noticed the dream, the eye, almost simultaneously. Upon waking one night I saw in the corner of the room, right side of my bed, a visitor who seemingly was only a darken stain. Upon my eyes adjusting to the dark I saw the true image, an eye with many lashes covering the iris like a mother protecting a child. In my fright I flipped on the overhead light and saw that the image remained, a true image, not a vision, a true an ugly thing.

The dreams continued to haunt me, after sleeping I found myself transported to a strange land of creatures, all of them simply existing, no thought of my presence. I came to recognize myself to be an observer, a man brought to observe as the eye had observed me. It seemed fair, an even sort of trade.

The dream shook me. I frequently awoke drenched in sweat, hoping not to come face to face with another being so large it could crush me under a crooked and gangly appendage. I was afraid of waking up. But then, there was always the comfort of the eye. I came to know it, like a stray cat finding refuge. I came to be familiar with beings unknown to modern science. I came to be familiar with life outside of Earth itself and life outside reality. I came to know details of the place I was transported to. In the dream language was given and I came to know the name VIQA.

This word, VIQA was repeated to me in dream and stuck on my lips like flies to web. Then came other names, BUJE, OXAK, TIRVEL, all names foreign. I came to repeat these names, to chant them, to sleep peacefully under the influence of an all mighty eye, the eye connected to a foreign land of strange insectoid, building shaped, creatures of unknown origin, with abilities to transport knowledge into the mind of a simple Earth man.

Simple is the word of importance, perhaps my simplicity of nature granted me favor in their eye, as I have never been a questioning man. I have always gone along to get along and to live my life as peaceful as any other man should want to live. Perhaps this is why I was chosen?

With this language on my tongue and eyes shut close, I would carry out deeds for the beings. Sleepless nights were not sleepless, these nights were full of movement and as controlled the simple Earth man would go from home out into the world and do biddings of the beings. These biddings included kidnapping a child from a residence near, exploration of canine's guts, as well as samples from the bowels of a pregnancy. All these tasks I have done, but all these tasks were not done in right mind. They were performed in a controlled state of narcosis.

I can attest to this truth, as the idea of insanity has been run across in front of me by doctors and different men in suits. All the while all of them missing the eye in front of them, no, the eye in the corner of every room, simply looking ahead won't permit foreign vision. One must simply look ahead and be mindful of the corners, there the eye will peer and then you will see what the eye wants you to know.

If fortunate, one may even be transported, by way of dream, to the extra-terrestrial planet of unknown origin. There one may see truths and know of the words which inhabit the tongue like lovers from a yesteryear. Then will thou be transported to an all-white room devoid of sound or plaything, the whiteness like beams of transport. An all-white room, meant to block out visions, unknown to doctor's influence, the color of the creatures, information kept in mind.

When will Earth know the speech of the DEBWIN? I fear they've locked away their only conduit. What sayeth you, DEBWIN? Enhance my tongue and mind with the speech of your race, so that I may join with you in otherworldly knowledge.

Horse Cocoon (Tom Leaf)

Blake's transformation began one Thursday evening with a question, whispered from the shadowy back seat of his Volvo.

'Does this smell like chloroform to you?'

He struggled, briefly.

***

Julia Miller was snapped into dazed consciousness by an ammonia-soaked rag pressed to her face. She wondered why she could no longer feel her legs. A latex gloved hand moved her fringe to one side.

'You're doing fine. All things considered.'

Julia wanted to ask her husband why he was wearing a surgical mask on his day off, but her tongue drowsily refused to come unstuck from the roof of her cotton mouth. A large surgical lamp loomed over her; its chrome face angled out of view. She tried to sit up and failed, bound by three webbing straps pinning her to the bed. Julia knew she was naked and couldn't understand why a hospital gown hadn't been provided. She had a curiously overwhelming desire to lick her own genitals.

The lamp was turned on and its concave mirrored surface turned towards her.

'I've performed a rather extreme procedure on you.'

Julia furrowed her brow in confusion at her reflection. Ten nipples, a tuft of fur where her belly button should have been and a semi-erect penis with a lipstick red tip.

'That's not my penis.' she slurred, her fat tongue, now unstuck, lolling from the side of her mouth.

'It is now.'

***

Blake dangled over sawdust, pendulous strings of vomit hanging from his slack lips.

'Nausea is merely a side effect of the anaesthetic. It won't concern you for much longer, I can assure you.'

The voice was familiar and yet Blake was unable to turn his head to identify who was speaking. His neck, held firm as if encircled by a thick rubber collar, was swollen and he struggled to take anything other than shallow breaths. Beads of sweat ran off his fevered forehead, stinging his sleep crusted eyes.

"You have an increased body temperature. That is to be expected.'

Blake squinted at the plywood floor beneath him. He felt like a tortoise trapped within its shell, unable to lift or rotate his head in any direction. An immensely hot, soft weight pressed down upon him.

Any attempt to move was impossible; his arms and legs were worryingly unresponsive.

'Where the fuck am I?' Blake croaked, his throat rough with bile.

'Exactly where I want you. And, please, mind your language. Vulgarity is always so unnecessary.'

The voice, cultured and calm.

'Miller? S'that you?'

'Correct. Please don't attempt to struggle, there is no point.'

Blake's eyes swivelled wildly in his head, trying to catch sight of the other man. Miller dropped to one knee, the pale blue cotton of his neatly pressed slacks smearing Blake's freshly glistening vomit.

'There we are, eye to eye, at last.' Miller's breath smelt of whisky. Blake's did not.

'You are in my wife's horsebox, strung up in an equine strap hammock.'

Miller reached forward and painfully squeezed Blake's sweat sheened cheek between a well-manicured thumb and forefinger.

'Don't get too comfortable. This won't take long.' Blake's bowels filled with ice.

'Let's talk about you and Julia.'

'That wasn't me.' Blake whispered, struggling to fight back the panic in his voice. Miller raised his eyebrows in mock surprise.

'The camera never lies, old chap, and my surgery is bristling with 'em. Saw you both, clear as day, on the old CCTV, on many an occasion.'

'No. Listen, I can explain…'

'Have the bloody balls to admit it. You and her, *in flagrante delicto*, bang to rights, etc.'

Miller moved out of sight. Blake could hear him dragging something heavy across the sawdust covered floor of the horsebox. Sunlight arrowing in from the translucent plastic roof flashed back into Blake's squinting eyes as Miller slid a full-length mirror underneath the hammock. Blake couldn't make sense of the reflection. His own scared face, peeking out from what looked like a bulging sandbag, draped on either side by a blue tarpaulin.

'The whole operation took over thirteen hours,' Miller said, 'and all on my lonesome, due to the highly irregular nature of it. Bloody knackered at the end of it. Still, I think you'll agree it was worth it in the end.'

Miller reached out of view of the mirror, moving around and behind Blake, unhooking the tarpaulin until, finally released, it dropped to the floor.

'What do you think, old man? Not bad, is it?'

Not a sandbag, then. Something much worse. Blake screamed, then vomited once more before falling into a dead faint.

***

Blake stirred, woken by the smell of horse shit and vomit.

'Wake up, you fool. I need you to pay attention.'

73

Miller slapped him hard, first on one cheek then the other.

'Where am I?'

The mirror beneath Blake had been taken away. Above him, the heat and the immense weight still bore down.

'You're here because of Julia. It's always been about Julia. Julia and her horse or Julia and her dog. Treated them like bloody fashion accessories, swanning around the village either on top of one or leading the other. Silly cow.'

Miller crouched down, staring into Blake's face with eyes as black and soulless as a shark.

'Four months ago you came along. Another accessory, another trophy to be paraded.'

Miller stood, moving out of sight.

'You're inside a horse. My wife's horse to be exact. Can't remember its name, exactly. Starlight or Spangle or something typically feminine and pointless, like that.'

The smell of horse shit. The sheer weight upon him.

'Human and equine anatomies aren't that different – it's just a question of scale. Had to break a couple of her ribs to slide you in. Obviously, had to remove your ribcage completely otherwise you wouldn't have compressed enough to fit the space.'

Blake listened in horror, eyes wildly staring. Above and behind him, a thick, fluttering movement had begun to ripple across the length of his body.

'No need to retain the ends of your arms and legs, they just got in the way, so they've gone the way of all flesh. Pardon the pun.'

The movement, more rhythmic and regular now, was increasing in intensity, growing stronger with each passing second.

'Your thighs and upper arms were needed to stop you slopping about inside like a cock in a sock, so they're fused with steel pins to the old girl's humerus and femur bones. Sliced open the thick musculature of her chest, poked your head out through the gap and formed a seal by double stitching your neck skin back in place. Head between the filly's bulging chest. There's a sweet irony in that, don't you think?'

Miller slid the full-length mirror back in place.

Blake's head, pathetically small, crowning from the mare's chest was the only human evidence of the abomination that Miller had created. Beneath Blake, the thick powerful forelegs of the horse hung suspended six inches off the floor of the horsebox. Above him, the neck and head of the horse could not be seen but he sensed the physical immensity of the animal.

'The sedative is wearing off now and she's jammed to the gills with amphetamine.' Miller explained. 'S he's absolutely raring to go. '

The undulating movement of the horse's internal organs intensified, no longer pacified by the anaesthetic. Blake could feel the animal coming to life around him, the hot liquid reality of it pressing upon him on all sides, wrapping him in its blood

75

hot, fleshy coils. Heart, lungs, liver and stomach folding, pulsing, wet and heavy, driven by the constant thunderous thump of the animal's heartbeat. Flickering shivers undulated across the skin of its chest, fluttering against Blake's cheek and its breath, hot and rapid blew across his face, the scent sweetly reminiscent of sun kissed pastures and warm hay.

'I've pumped her full of enough painkillers to last for the short time you'll be together. I have made no such provision for you, I'm afraid. Empty your bowels and bladder as much as you like, any waste will trickle into the gaps between her organs. You won't need any nutrition – you won't need it where you're going.'

Miller moved towards the back of the horsebox and dropped the loading ramp. Sunlight streamed in and a fresh breeze stirred the sawdust on the floor. Miller swept his arms wide, indicating the landscape before him.

'Miller's Chase. Fifty-three acres of beautiful English pasture, a verdant valley flanked on either side by dark ancient woodland. Been in the family for generations.'

The snap of a buckle. An impatient whinny.

'Best of all is the view at the end. A sheer drop to the ocean and nothing beyond that until you get to France. Wonderfully scenic. Spent many a boyhood summer here.'

Miller paused, lost in wistful reminiscence.

'Anyway,' he continued, releasing a second and third buckle, 'cometh the hour and all that.'

The fourth and final buckle was released.

The horse, freed of the harness, dropped to its knees.

'And ... we're off.' screamed Miller, punching the horse's flank.

***

Miller woke with a start.

Something was in the house.

Three floors below him, beyond the spidery limit of the twisting staircase, something had scuttled into life.

He could hear rapid movement within the dark ocean of the hallway: an erratic clattering across the parquet floor, a skittering towards the bottom of the staircase.

And then silence.

Miller said nothing. He could think of nothing to say. He wanted to say something, to make some noise of his own, to take control. But he was afraid of what might come to his call.

He sat up, fumbling for the light switch.

Suddenly, it came; a barking, screaming, whinnying roar, tearing the air apart.

Miller shrieked.

'Christ! Who's there? Who are you?'

For a moment there was no further sound except the thud of Miller's heartbeat, thundering in his ear. A slight breeze drifted up the staircase, ozone rich and thick with the scent of dark, wet things. The bottom stair creaked; whatever had

77

moved in the darkness now began to climb, its progress slow and ponderous. Each slouching step seemed familiar.

Clip, clop.

Like castanets, like coconut shells. The first-floor landing, now breached, groaned under the intruder's monstrous weight.

'No, you're not real.' Miller whispered, eyes wide with fear, the light switch forgotten. He stared slack jawed into the granular darkness beyond his bedroom door.

Two floors below the thing waited, listening, then continued to climb, dead steps echoing off the stairwell walls, rhythmic and terrifying.

Clip, clop.

Clip, clop.

The timber floorboards of the second-floor landing squeaked in protest.

Clip.

Clop.

The terror that lurked beyond the final curve of the staircase was still unseen and yet, Miller knew. He knew what had come for him, and offered up a whispered prayer, an old wife's tale, repeated like a mantra.

'A horse can't climb a staircase. A horse can't climb a staircase. A horse can't …'

***

Miller, paralysed with fear, stared in mute horror at the abomination that stumbled into view

78

before him. That which had once been a horse and that which had once been a man, were biologically entwined and yet so horrifically broken they barely resembled the sum of their parts. The creature tottered on flesh stripped, splintered legs, barely able to support its stinking bulk. Its head, partially severed in the fall, smeared backwards along the line of its mane, the face blindly buried in a nest of wet tendons that hung from a ragged gash in its neck; the hide was split by countless lipped wounds that vomited forth grey, glistening ropes of muscle, providing a rich feeding ground for the dozens of seaweed encrusted spider crabs swarming and multiplying over the twisted length of the creature's body.

And there, leering grotesquely from the lacerated flesh of the dead mare's chest was Blake, face bloated with sea water, his blind gaze blank and pitiless, for the fish had taken his eyes. The dead mare stumbled forward and leaned against the door frame, pressing forward. Blake craned his face further still, his slack jaws dropped open and he screamed.

A piercing, spiralling, penny whistle siren of a scream, a foghorn, cavern echo, bellow of a scream that punched the air and rattled the bedroom windows.

Miller shrieked, wrapped himself in sweat-soaked sheets, clasped his hands tightly to his face and curled into a foetal position. Unwittingly, he'd emptied his bowels.

Almost as suddenly, the screaming stopped. Miller lay perfectly still, swaddled in shame and shit, hot mess pooling around his bony ankles.

Silence.

He peered through his fingers; the room was empty. Blake and the mare, both gone. Miller sat up. He could see through his bedroom door to the gloomy landing beyond. A nightmare. Yes, it had to be. No other explanation. He let out a shuddering sigh of relief.

The creature rose noiselessly from beside the bed; Miller caught a brief glimpse of the terror towering over him before he was snuffed out like a candle, his final moments fittingly violent.

The frenzied attack that followed, the horrific manner in which Miller was taken apart, kicked into mush, splashed to the four walls, was chaotic. And yet, beyond the remote red brick walls of the Georgian house, beyond its moon-washed ornamental lawns and far beyond the tree lined lane that eventually wound towards Miller's Chase there were no witnesses to the reduction of Miller.

Except one.

In the stables, tucked into the cobwebbed corner of a straw lined stall, shackled to a wall beneath a hand carved sign that read 'Stardust', the dog woman hybrid previously identifying as Julia Miller cowered in mute terror trying, and failing, to cross its bull terrier paws over its Botox plumped, lipstick smeared face.

In The Detail (Liam A. Spinage)

Letitia stood alone on the balcony, glass in hand, looking out over the night sky. Far below her was the swirling fog of city lights: neon signs, headlamps, streetlights, Mere pinpricks at this distance but they melded together in a medley of memories. There had been times when she had been behind one of those lights, like so many other people in the city and not detached from it here in the penthouse. She swirled the champagne in the flute, sending bubbles scattering like flies. The sweet glass of victory twinkled in the suffused glow of the apartment lighting and the candle she had precariously balanced on the balcony table next to her, sputtering in the breeze but remaining defiant. She felt a lot of empathy for that candle. A tiny, exhaustible flicker of passion against a sky of brooding, monotonous darkness.

Still lost in thought, she took a tentative sip, relishing the cool feeling as it trickled down her throat. The rest of the bottle sat on the table next to the candle, still chilling in the ice bucket. She would save that for later. There were reasons to celebrate tonight, but the past five years had installed in her a certain degree of caution. Not for the first time but maybe - just maybe - for the last, she reflected on that momentous decision five years ago which had fundamentally changed her life.

The door buzzer sounded from deep within the apartment. She paused for a moment, but the buzzer did not. She usually had someone to deal with these interruptions, but she had dismissed her staff for the evening so she would not be disturbed, Except by him, obviously, though she hadn't thought he would approach in such a mundane way. A puff of smoke, maybe, a whiff of sulphur, a flash of bright flame. No, he was about to enter in the same way that everyone else did.

She reached towards the white marble table and delicately deposited her glass there. Then she began to make her way back through her spacious lodgings. A four-poster bed with white satin drapes and twinkling dimmed fairy lights for that otherworldly feel. A spotless lounge, floored in white polished marble and a single small but perfectly placed rug. Busts of Medea, Circe and Ariadne sourced from the finest auction houses in the city and the world beyond. An entry room with a spacious cloakroom to one side, hidden behind black velvet curtains. Effortlessly, she raised a manicured finger and released the latch. As the handle turned, she paced back into the lounge and struck a pose on the scarlet chaise longue opposite the overstuffed armchair. That was the single item of furniture which stuck out in her otherwise immaculately appointed paradise and it was here for a reason. It was the only memory she allowed herself from her former life. Until now.

She could hear his footsteps and the click of his cane approaching. *Something wicked this way comes.* A moment of rustling where he had clearly divested himself of an outer garment in the allotted place, A rushing intake of breath as he surveyed the sheer majesty of what he had helped her to afford. As he approached, Letitia faltered for a moment. His very presence drew her back to that time when they had first met, when the power difference between them had been so very different. The sheer malignancy of that shadow, even when dressed in human form, drew her in like a moth to a flame. For the first time, she began to wonder whether the strategy she had devised would work. She shivered, trembled even, at every footstep until she glimpsed herself momentarily in the mirror and saw her younger self, high on life, drunk on her own confidence, about to make what could easily be the biggest and most dangerous mistake of her life. She barely recognised that young girl in herself after all this time. She was different now. Not just richer, but more mature, more experienced. Her inner confidence grew and she regained her composure just as he spoke to her,

"Good evening. I see you were expecting me." His voice, low but sonorous, more than a hint of mischief, as it had been five years ago.

Finally, she turned to meet his face. Though she was sure it was just the same after all this time, the balance between them had shifted slightly. That face had haunted and taunted her over the years, reflected in dozens of shop windows, revolving doors, cocktail glasses, champagne flutes. Was it just her imagination or had he been with her every step of the way, looking, laughing, crowing, waiting… Just how much of her life did he know?

The face was still long and lean. In the light of the bar where they had first met, it had been sweaty, sallow even, yet still handsome. That's what had first attracted her to him. His lashes, his moustaches. There were few well-groomed and well-dressed individuals in that dive. She had instantly wanted to know his story. He, in turn, had instantly wanted to know hers. The night had passed slowly, exchanges between them became more friendly, more fervent. Then, as she gazed into his hypnotising grey eyes, he had made her an offer she couldn't refuse. "Hello, you old devil. Has it really been five years?"

His face was different now, she realised. The line of his lips which had once been so willing to laugh now formed a sneer, giving way as he spoke to betray the immense hunger behind those perfect white teeth. She instinctively gulped, trying not to show it. If she showed fear now, all would be lost.

"It has. As you well know. And now I arrive at the appointed hour to collect what is due. I see that you have been enjoying your gift." He extended an arm sleeved in a dark suit - charcoal grey, she thought in the dim light, with a flash of bright red lining - as a sweep around the penthouse.

"I have not forgotten. Please, sit." She gestured at the cracked leather of the armchair. He bowed slightly, mockingly, and did so.

"I'm here to collect, waitress."

She laughed, deep and rich and long. He joined in.

"It's been a long time since I've been that, but still, I have a memory of that night when we first met, see? You're sitting on it. That's the armchair from the staff break room where you sat as I poured out my hopes and fears and you offered me the world on a plate. A simple transaction, really." Was it her imagination or did he actually begin to look uncomfortable? Had he perhaps an inkling of what was about to happen?

"I recall it well, waitress."

Well. To be addressed in that manner a second time was simply rude. Not that she considered the devil above petty manipulation, far from it. He was trying to put her off-kilter. Playing with his food before he devoured her utterly.

"Do you also recall..." she tailed off, lost for a moment in the handsomeness of his lean face, those hungry eyes, that perfect chin. "Do you recall what it was I asked of you?"

"I do, but I don't need to. It's all here." From the interior of his suit jacket, he withdrew a single piece of paper and let it unfurl, first from his wrist to the arm of the chair and then across the floor, stopping finally at the outline of the rug. "Second thoughts, waitress? It's a little too late for that. Five years too late, I should say. Don't be coy. You accepted the gift, now accept the consequences." He leaned forward in a gesture of quiet menace clearly honed by what she imagined was millennia of practice. Behind him on the wall, his shadow loomed large even while he remained seated. Though her rooms were lit with the brightest lamps, the shadow he cast now - and the shadow he had cast over her life for the last five years - threatened to drown her in darkness.

"Yes. Success. That's what I traded my soul for. Success in my chosen occupation. And that has worked out very well for me, very well indeed, I must agree. I have the world at my feet." She stood quietly, in one lithe movement, her pearls swaying slowly at her alabaster throat.

"There must be a particular thirst for cocktails that I was unaware of at the time. Who would have thought!"

She moved in stockinged feet to the scroll now fully unfurled across the room and removed an elegant pair of glasses from a case in her purse. He seemed to anticipate this move.

"They always think there's something in the contract that can get them out." This was barely perceptible to Letitia, almost a mutter, but it echoed nevertheless around the empty space between them and hung, lingering in the air with a faint whiff of threat and sulphur. He spoke it as if an aside to a hidden third party. Or perhaps to himself, a mote of contempt for his victims which he had only vocalised so that she could feel the cruel, casual mockery in his voice.

"Oh, I'm sure many have tried!" She attempted a laugh, but it came out a little hoarse, a little stilted. He was beginning to sense her fear. "It's quite clear though, you're right." She knelt down before the

86

lengthy contract and squinted briefly at the small print before beginning to read the first line. "I, Letitia Maria de Santis do, on this day of November 27th 1981, at the hour of 3 AM, enter into this agreement whereby I will be granted unparalleled success in my chosen profession for five years in return for which at the appointed hour five years from now I will relinquish my soul to the devil in payment." She shot a glance across at him over the rim of her glasses delicately balanced on the bridge of her nose. On the mantle, perched between two alabaster busts, a golden clock ticked slowly, irrevocably, towards that very hour.

"So?" He rubbed his hands together in glee. "What are we waiting for?"

"It's the small print that interests me."

"Oh?" He appeared unperturbed. "Most people don't even give that a second glance. I mean, what's a few extra words in comparison to five years of fame and riches?"

"Is it always five years?" The question seemed to shock him a little and he tilted his head a little, his brows raised quizzically.

"It is traditional, yes. Just enough rope for people to hang themselves with, you see. Oh, I know..." here he brushed off a little yellow dust from his shoulder as easily as he brushed off her question. "I know that fifteen minutes of fame was all the rage some while back, but what we savour is the anticipation of doom that a contract end represents. Why, you wouldn't believe the lengths some people go to trying to get out of the deal. Or maybe you would?" At that last line, the inflection in his voice changed slightly, becoming more contemplative. Then he laughed again and the moment was lost. "You're not trying to negotiate an extension, are you? Oh, how simply delightful It won't work, I'm afraid."

"And yet there is nothing here in any of the subclauses which necessarily precludes such an arrangement, I thought it at least worth a try."

"Sorry." He was not sorry. He was not an entity for which remorse, repentance or forgiveness could even exist. The word was a mere formality, an amuse-bouche to whet his appetite before his lean form sprang forward, pouncing voraciously on his trapped prey. "But when your number's up…"

"Yes, I understand." She got back to her feet and walked over to a cabinet on the far side of the room and flinging open the doors. "Still, it seems that at least I can offer you a drink while you're here." The chair creaked as he turned it around slightly, arching his back to take in the full display of bottles available. There must have been over a hundred, all manner of shapes and sizes, antique bottles covered in dust, cut glass carafes full of unknown concoctions, shiny new bottles of the most expensive spirits affordable on earth.

"I will take one cocktail of your choosing to humour you. After all, when you've been instrumental in making the career of the finest cocktail waitress in the world, it's a bonus to see what you have helped achieve."

"Very well. Allow me." Letitia busied herself for some moments, unstopping some bottles and inspecting the contents. Finally, she began pouring small measures into a cocktail shaker and then reached into the cabinet and extracted two highball glasses. He seemed content to watch her in those silent moments, savouring the last hours of her life before he claimed it for eternity.

She thought turning her back on him - especially at such a critical juncture - might have been perceived as a power move. Certainly, Letitia could feel her power growing, though her hands still shook slightly as she uncorked a large bottle of fortified wine. Perhaps, just perhaps, this might actually work. She hid her fear but nevertheless wanted to know how he saw her at that moment. Was she still prey? Or, just maybe, boon companion? Dare she even imagine… adversary?

She could see him out of the corner of her eye, just about, but more keenly in the many reflective surfaces of the bottles arrayed before her. His lean figure, at ease in the armchair, his eager face watching her back, reflected and distorted by the different folds and twists in the antique bottles which lined the cabinet. His visage tinted blue here, green there from the contents of those bottles, elongated almost beyond recognition by the cut of the crystal decanters, fractured into multiple facades by the refraction of the light through the water, each proffering a different promise. But in each of them, clear as anything, were the glint of those grey, uncompromising, all-seeing eyes.

Finally, her task complete, she added an olive and a twist to each, then made her way back to the chaise longue. She leaned over and proffered him one of the glasses with a final flourishing swirl. The clear liquid sprang into life as hues of red and yellow began swirling around each other as if in mutual pursuit.

"Very clever!" He raised the glass to his ruby lips, taking in the heady aroma. Letitia mirrored the procedure.

"To us! Success at a price."

"To us!"

He took his first swallow of whatever deliciousness she had prepared, Letitia herself hesitated for a moment before she swallowed, waiting to see his reaction,

He began spluttering almost immediately, the liquid spraying from his mouth as he started to cough, Letitia looked over, knowingly.

"What have you done? That was awful! Probably the worst thing I've ever tasted!" When he had recovered a little of his form, he reached into his jacket for a slate-grey silk handkerchief which, she noted, was even monogrammed with a little red 'L' in the corner. He held it to his lips, still occasionally retching, and wiped the spittle from his chin,

"I never was any good at making cocktails."

"What? I made you the best in the world! What have you done with that? How have you got all this wealth from so little talent?"

90

"I direct you again to the terms of our contract."

"I... What? You wanted to be the best at your chosen profession. What happened?"

"Correct. But that chosen profession wasn't making cocktails. I was only doing that to make ends meet during my studies. My chosen profession was contract law." She sipped at her own cocktail, unstirred and looked back at him with an expression half-grimace, half-grin. "I do apologise if that happens to be a matter of confusion for you. The way the contract is worded wasn't specific about that, you see." She leaned forward conspiratorially, confident in her approach now. "But we can change that, you and I."

He could feel the power between them shifting slightly. He didn't like it.

"I'm quite sure I don't know what you mean."

"I mean that it's still possible for me to negotiate an extension. Now, you, as the party of the first part..."

"Wait, wait." He seemed to need time to think. Letitia thought this was amusing and her mouth betrayed the tiniest of smirks. But it wasn't over yet. Even as the balance between them began to tip in her favour, she couldn't afford to let it show fully. Still, she enjoyed watching him squirm as she swilled the contents of her glass. When she saw her own reflection in that glass and his too, hovering on the edge, she was struck at the similarity between them. She looked up.

"Why wait? By accident, it seems that you have created the finest contract lawyer on earth. That's what has brought me all this fame, all these lovely curios, this wonderful penthouse apartment. You thought I got all this from inventing some new drink? Please. If I understand correctly - and here the print is quite clear - when I go with you then all this is over. All the gifts offered, this keen mind, this knowledge, are lost to me and you both. It's also clear that despite all rumour to the contrary, hell really does not have all the best lawyers. There are clauses here that are so ridiculously archaic as to be meaningless. Surely you would appreciate my insights into it before you take your prize back with you for an infinity of torture?"

As pitches go, she thought she'd nailed it. He seemed to agree, but then a wry smile took over his face again. "What you suggest should take no more than five hours, let alone five more years. Nevertheless, I concur. Fix me something that's actually palatable and let us both take a look at the fine print together. Maybe you really can teach this old dog some new tricks."

Three hours later, they looked up from a second contract, with even more confounding legalese and clauses than the devil could hope for. Vials of red and black ink lie strewn across the cold marble of the floor and the teak writing desk; a feather had escaped from a quill and was slowly meandering across the floor toward the balcony in a breeze-borne bid for freedom.

"Well." He stood straight and tall. "That is certainly an improvement. I cannot thank you enough."

Letitia raised a single perfectly plucked eyebrow. He laughed. "A mere figure of speech, something I am certain never to write down." He sobered again and extended a long bony hand toward her. "Now, come. You are done with this world."

"Oh, I don't think so." Letitia drained a tiny cup heavy with caffeine stains. She also stood, stretching as she did so. For the first time, she looked him in the eye and did not blink. Then she picked up her contract again and slowly crossed the space between them, her stockinged feet silent on the marble floor. "The devil may be in the detail, but this line of the contract is just heavenly." She pursed her lips to proffer a kiss into the air. "*In return for which, at the appointed hour*. I'm afraid to break it to you, but that appointed hour has come and gone." Her eyes flicked briefly back to the clock on the mantle.

Letitia handed him the contract which he started at, dumbfounded, as she moved lithely across the room, stopping in front of her bedroom door. "It is now eight in the morning." With that, she threw open the door with a flourish, flooding the room with light from the balcony beyond. "The sun has risen while you made work for my idle hands. All those extra clauses. Dear me. I'll have to leave you now." She squinted through the door to her bedroom and the balcony where the sun had risen magnificently. "I have an appointment with another morning star. I'm sure you can find your own way out."

Letitia left the devil howling in frustrated rage, Letitia walked out into the light and poured herself another glass of champagne. She never had liked cocktails.

Chain Mail (Rickey Rivers Jr.)

1.

He's in the mail truck now, judging me, the mailman, the forever judge, smiling, pretending to be friendly. He waves like any other, with the same attire, but my neighborhood mailman is different.

To be a mailman is voyeuristic. This one for sure has spied. I remember taking a long hard look at him one day and a sick smile crept across his face. He winked at me, a knowing wink. My mail comes to my home unopened, but still, I know the truth. It's the look he gives. He knows my orders. He knows what I owe on bills. He's read my magazines. It's about privacy, the lack of it and his access to everything. He puts on a happy face so you can't see the malice hiding within. He knows me. He hates me. He's judging my purchases.

I've thought about the possibility of x-ray vision, implants hidden behind his eyes. Maybe that's how he's able to know? Technology's advancing. Who knows what government employees can do? Intel on my mail or your mail can easily be shared. There are no laws against reading unopened mail.

I go back and forth with perverse thoughts, the idea, how perverse it really is. A sick minded person who should serve the people instead works directly against them. Today is the day, though, the day for confrontation. I've decided to speak to him, one on one. It's time for the important questions.

***

It's noon now and I wait. He should be here soon. When he arrives I'll catch him in the lie. Then we'll know.

The engine of the mail truck is easily recognizable. You can hear it from down the street. You just have to pay attention, shut off all the noise of music and others' vehicles, just take a moment to listen, really listen, soon enough you can recognize the sound of anything. Shush away the chirping birds, the barking dogs, really listen. Then you'll know.

***

I hear it. The mail truck is five houses down. I wait near the window. Four houses down. Now three, then two, then one, the mail truck stops by the mail box then rushes pass just as I dart outside. No mail today? Fine, but the mailman continues down the street driving past both neighbors on the right and taking a hard turn to the next street. He knew. He knew I was waiting.

I run to the garage but stop myself short. There's no reason to chase him. Tomorrow is another day. No, tomorrow is Sunday. There's no mail tomorrow. But that's okay, I'll wait.

***

It's Sunday and I'm sick. I'm in bed nearly the whole day. I'm in and out of the bathroom. I'm eating food I don't like and refusing to leave home. I have to wait here until it's time, finally time to see the mailman. I go from the living room through the hallway into the bedroom pacing. I can't contain myself.

Sleep was bad. I can't sleep when I'm angry. I lift weights. I take a protein shake out of the fridge and pass by the living room window. That's when I see him again. He's outside in the white mail truck and he's right by the mailbox. He's looking at me. How long has he been there? We lock eyes. I drop my protein shake and run to the front door. The mailman speeds down the street. This time head on, past a red light. He's fast in that truck.

After cleaning up the protein shake in the kitchen I think of calling my local post office on Monday. Then I rethink. There's no use. They're in on it, of course. You can't trust your government anymore. Times have changed. It's been a long time since the government cared about people. People were secondary. Machines were the future.

I look at the kitchen clock. It's almost evening. Tomorrow can't come soon enough.

2.

It's Monday. I keep the front door unlocked. When he's two houses down I'll approach. That's the

97

plan. I realize at this moment I don't actually know what I'll do when I talk to him. What can I say?

"I know you've been reading my mail!"

He'll think I'm insane. I have to be rational. I go to the kitchen, search the drawers and find a knife. This will only be a last resort. I don't intend to use it. I understand that you can't hurt a government employee. I won't hurt him unless I have to.

***

It's 3 PM. I hear the engine. He's a few houses down. I look outside the window. I can't see him but I know the engine sound. I wait a few seconds then I see the sun's glare off the top of the mail truck. He's four houses down. I stand behind the front door and listen to the sound of the engine turn off and back on again. He's three houses down. I clutch the door handle. My hands are sweaty. The mail truck engine cuts on and off. He's two houses down.

I open the front door and head out. Speed walking, I head to the mailbox. The mail truck engine starts and stops short. He saw me. The mail truck pulls forward, stops and the mailman puts mail into the mailbox of the house on my left. Then it's my turn.

The engine of the mail truck starts again and the mailman pulls forward. I wait for him to slow down but he speeds up instead. I leap toward the open window and climb inside. The mail man's eyes are forward. I'm holding on. He knows it.

"Look at me!" I yell. But his eyes are forward and he's speeding by houses.

"UNATHORIZED PASSANGER IN THE VEHICLE" A mechanical voice speaks from somewhere in the truck, the radio?

I pull myself in as best I can. The mailman looks at me with a cold glare. "Sir," he says, "this is the wrong truck."

"Stop looking..." I manage, wanting to say more, the almost pre-recorded lines I said to myself time and time again. *Stop looking at my mail. Stop reading my bills.*

Cars are honking as we ride further and further down the street. He's taken a few risky turns, trying to knock me out of the vehicle. But I'm strong enough to hold on... to something.

I realize what I'm holding onto: the metallic body inside the mail truck. The mailman's legs are bound to it. He's almost wielded to the truck. I feel woozy. I've seen him leave the truck before. So why now am I seeing his feet bound to truck, hands fused to the steering wheel, skin resembling the shade of engine parts? I'm blacking out. I remember the knife, but it doesn't matter now. I hear a loud screech and a sound like a scream from outside the truck. We're crashing, it's loud.

***

I hear noise around me. People are talking. Then I hear sirens, footsteps. I'm hurt. I look around. I'm still in the truck. The metal fused mailman's gaze is on me, but his inhuman eyes have faded. I try to move, but I can't. My body hurts.

A policeman, perhaps a special one, is yelling into the vehicle. He says my name. How does he know my name? He repeats my name, but I can't answer him. I think I have broken bones. My jaw hurts.

***

There's a bunch of noise around me now and I can't see. I hear a drill, maybe a circular saw, a scraping sound. Someone's walking on metal.

"Let's get him out."

Good, someone's helping. But I'm not in the street. This place feels secluded. Beyond the sounds of workmen I hear an echo. We're in a building.

***

"Let's test him out."

I look around and there's metal, nothing but. A console sits in front of me. Then I see the steering wheel. I can't move. I look down. My legs are not my legs. They are similar to the metal parts in the current cage I'm sitting in. Yes, a cage. There's a door to my right and one to my left.

"Load up the truck!

I Waited For You (Thomas M. Malafarina)

Based on a work of art of the same title by Niall Parkinson

"Guilt is cancer. Guilt will confine you, torture you, destroy you as an artist.
It's a black wall. It's a thief." - Dave Grohl

"Guilt is perhaps the most painful companion of death." - Coco Chanel

Robert woke with a start, hearing his smartphone vibrating on the nightstand. In one clumsy motion, he swung his feet out from under the covers, sat upright and looked around him.

He staggered over to a doorway in the unfamiliar bedroom, which he hoped would lead to a hallway and in turn might get him to a bathroom. He found the bathroom and stumbled in, still naked, and dropped his clothes in a heap on the worn linoleum floor. Under even the best of conditions, the phone call would have devastated him, but he physically felt like crap right now, which was a perfect match to how he felt emotionally.

Robert splashed cold water onto his face then used some more to wet his hair. He made a feeble attempt to finger comb the unruly mess since he could not find a comb or brush. The bathroom was filthy, looked as if it hadn't been cleaned in months. Women's clothing was scattered about and undergarments seemed to hang from almost every possible place available. He managed to dig under some random supplies and found a tube of toothpaste but no brush. So again, making good use of his digits, he did his best to finger-brush his teeth.

He knew the intense tasting toothpaste would do little to mask his morning breath which was savory with remnants of the previous night's binge, but he had no time; he had to get moving. He had finally gotten 'the call' and that meant there was no time to waste. Robert hurriedly threw on his underwear and then his pants and shirt, doing his best to make himself look presentable. He could at the phone's display for a millisecond before pressing the 'ACCEPT' icon and answering with a gruff, sleepy "Hello?" The name displayed had been Sunny Rest.

"Mr. Nelson?" The professional sounding voice on the other end of the line said. Robert felt the bed move slightly as the woman lying next to him tossed, mumbled something unintelligible, farted and then apparently fell back to sleep.

Robert rolled his eyes in disgust and replied into the phone, "Yes. This is Robert Nelson. Is everything all right?"

The voice on the other end said, "It's time, Mr. Nelson. You had better get over here as quickly as possible. She said she is waiting for you, but I'm afraid she has little time left."

"I'll be right there," Robert said. He disconnected the call while gathering his various articles of clothing strewn all about the floor. He bent to pick up his underwear and felt a whiskey-induced belch rising in his throat. He suppressed it, feeling it might be vomit. He could taste the previous night's alcohol churning inside him, he preferred to keep it down if at all humanly possible. YYYYYYYYY

only find one sock, so he threw it on the floor, slipped his shoes over bare feet and hurried back out into the hall.

"Hey... where the hell are you sneaking off to?" A slurred, husky voice spoke from down the hall. It was ... it was ... his bedmate from the previous night ... whatever her name might be. He wasn't surprised to realize he had absolutely no idea. She was standing naked in the hallway, leaning on the bedroom doorframe, smoking a cigarette. She looked a lot older, a lot less attractive and a lot more haggard than she had appeared the night before. The saying 'road hard and put away wet' flashed through his mind.

"Gotta go." Robert said, continuing toward the stairs, "Family emergency."

"Call me," the woman called after him, making the hand gesture of index finger and pinky up to the side of her wrinkled face.

"I will," he replied, knowing full well that would never happen. He seldom called any of these women, even on those rare occasions when he did remember their names.

He rushed out the front door of the row house, not having the slightest idea where he was. He looked around and found his car parked near the curb halfway up the block. He realized he was somewhere in the city and no matter where that might be, Robert had to get to Sunny Rest as soon as he possibly could.

He drove out of the unfamiliar city neighborhood and saw signs for the bypass. Once there, he'd find his way easily. On his way out of the city, he thought briefly about the woman whose bed he had just fled. How many had there been in the last month or so? He couldn't recall and didn't want to. There was no joy to be gained from such recollections, no pleasant memories of sexual conquests, only gut-wrenching guilt.

His mind was swimming with a myriad of disjointed thoughts. He was still hungover and now he was heading to Sunny Rest likely for the last time. There had been many false alarms, but somehow deep inside, Robert knew this was the real deal. The guilt he felt about the place he had just left was tied directly to where he was heading. He was going to see Cindy, his wife of more than thirty years and the one true love of his life.

Cindy was in Sunny Rest Hospice Center and she was dying. She had been dying for the past year. Despite his actions, Robert truly loved his wife and their marriage had been one of the few successful ones. It all seemed so unfair. Most of their friends were divorced, separated, or stayed together in rotten marriages for the children's sake. But his and

Cindy's had been one for the record books, at least until cancer struck.

Her decline had been quick, only two months earlier Cindy had been permanently hospitalized, needing round-the-clock care. Two weeks ago, Robert had been told the end was near and Cindy would have to go into Sunny Rest Hospice Center. The hospitalization devastated Robert. They had both known she was terminal during the past year and they did all they could to get her affairs in order. They'd even sold their large home and moved into a small apartment and got Robert ready for his life alone. One of the things Robert found so distressing was how they had spent far too much of her last year preparing for her imminent death.

Robert had tried his best to hold it together after Cindy was hospitalized. Still, after two weeks of barely sleeping and wandering throughout the lifeless apartment at night, he went to his employer and requested a leave of absence. His boss agreed since Robert could not focus on his duties any longer and the man decided he should be spending what time remained with Cindy.

The first few weeks in the hospital Robert and Cindy spent their days holding hands and reliving their past life even but as Cindy's pain increased, so did the number of medicines required to suppress it. Soon Cindy was spending most of their time together sleeping. Robert stayed by her side as she continued to lose weight and wither away to nothing right before his eyes. These weeks caused Robert to plunge into a deep unbearable depression, the likes of which he had never experienced in his life.

Robert knew he had to do something, anything to distract his thoughts from Cindy's worsening condition, or he surely would go mad. However, no matter what he tried, it just didn't seem to help. Finally, one night after spending the day watching his frail wife sleep almost nonstop, Robert stopped by a local bar on his way home. He couldn't stand the thought of facing the empty apartment again. He wasn't usually a drinking man but occasionally would have one with dinner back when he and Cindy could still go out to eat. But that night, he drank and he drank and damn if it didn't feel good. Several hours later, he wasn't thinking about Cindy or his problems any longer. He was barely capable of thinking at all.

Thus began a ritual which he practiced religiously night after night. Robert would awaken late in the morning and freshen up before going to the hospital. Not that it mattered because most of the day, Cindy was unresponsive. But he always took care to eliminate any tell-tale odors for those few lucid moments his wife had each day. He would spend his time with Cindy and then afterward would stop by a bar, drink until he was plastered, then go home, sleep it off and start all over the following day. Robert knew this was dangerous, bad for his health, but he didn't care any longer. All he wanted was to be completely numb.Then, after a week or two of this routine, something unexpected and disturbing happened.

Unknown to Robert at that time it would be, the first of many such occurrences. After following another night of binge drinking, he had awoken in a strange bed, naked, with an equally peculiar woman. He had no memory of how he had gotten there or what they had done. But regardless, he was riddled with guilt. He had never been unfaithful to his wife during their entire marriage and would have never even considered doing such a thing. And then it happened again and then again.

Soon it too became as much a part of his nightly ritual as the drinking had been. And the closer his wife got to death more guilt he felt about it. And the worse he felt, the more he drank. It was no longer just a vicious cycle but had become a downward spiral at an ever-increasing speed. Now it seemed like he woke up in some new bed with some unknown woman every morning and he had no idea how he had gotten there.

Now driving down the bypass, Robert saw the exit, which he knew would take him to Sunny Rest. Only a few minutes had passed, but it seemed like it had been a lifetime to Robert. He felt as if he had aged ten years in the past ten minutes. He haphazardly parked his car, raced to the entrance, then down the hall to the room where he knew Cindy awaited him for what would probably be the last time. His stomach was sick with grief as he walked into her dimly lit, quiet bedroom. As he approached the bed, a nurse walked by and gave him a disapproving look. He was taken aback, feeling as if this woman thought she had the right to judge him.

He looked over to his wife's deathbed and saw her emaciated form lying there, looking at him with eyes that seemed much too large for their sunken sockets. She was a living skeleton. Robert could tell she was aware the time of her passing was upon them and all he wanted to do was vomit. He couldn't come to grips with the fact that in just a few moments, his once beautiful wife would be dead. She weakly lifted her right arm and crooked a bony finger, indicating that he could come to her. She tried to raise her arms to hug him as he approached but was too weak, so he wrapped his arms gently about her skeletal frame.

Cindy's pale lips touched his ear and he heard her say, "I waited for you." Robert understood she was ready to pass on but wanted to say one last goodbye to him first, to tell him she loved him and to make sure he would be all right without her. But as Robert softly held her, he felt her body tense and become rigid. That was when he suddenly realized his tragic mistake.

In the past, Robert had always managed to shower, shave and adequately brush his teeth before visiting Cindy and most of those times, they rarely had the opportunity to be this close. But in his haste and stupor, Robert had forgotten to do this and now Cindy held him close, taking in all of the odors surrounding him; the foul stench of stale cigarettes, booze, sweat, cheap perfume and sex. She knew instantly what he had done.

Cindy released her weak grip on Robert and slid back down to the pillow. He stood staring lamely down into those once beautiful eyes. Cindy's face bore a look that seemed to encompass many emotions simultaneously; shock, disappointment, sorrow, grief, anger and even hatred. Here bulging eyes seemed to bore a hole right through Robert. They silently screamed, "How could you?" in his brain. Her pale lips began to tremble and in a raspy voice, she said, "I ... waited ... for ... YOU!" And then, a moment later, she died, her eyes losing focus but never breaking contact with Robert's desperate gaze.

Robert was heartsick, realizing not only that his wife was gone, but that instead of the peaceful passing they had always hoped for, the last living realization she had was that her husband was a lying, cheating, drunken whoremonger. His memory of their last moment together would be that he had been out partying with women while she lay dying, thinking only of him. Robert fell to his knees next to his wife's death bed and wept uncontrollably.

***

Robert sat on a chair in his tiny apartment which now seemed even more prominent than before, He sipped his whiskey on the rocks, already half-drunk at two in the afternoon, having just come back from burying his wife. The funeral had been a small, private affair with only a few friends and relatives in attendance. Robert and Cindy had no children, but a few nieces and nephews had stopped by to offer their condolences.

He wished it had been he who died and not Cindy. He could feel his guilt eating away at his insides as cancer had devoured his wife. And, worst of all, he was happy with the feeling. As far as he was concerned, there wasn't a death painful enough to make him suffer for what he had done to her. In the past, the alcohol had always managed to numb him and block out all his thoughts, but now it seemed to have the opposite effect. Now all he could think about was Cindy and how what he had done to her was beyond unforgiveness.

He clumsily lifted his glass to polish off the last of his whiskey when he noticed something strange on the wall across the room. It appeared to be a solitary black dot forming on the surface of the wall. Robert had no idea what might have been causing the stain, but he staggered over to the wall and sat down on the floor to get a closer look. By the time he arrived at the wall, a second dot had appeared. He stared at them, not having a clue what they might be.

Within a few seconds there were ten dots evenly spaced in two semi-circles. Then beneath the dots, two shapes began to form, appearing like the palms of two hands. They reminded Robert of when two hands are placed on the surface of a heavily fogged mirror and the area around the image even seemed to be liquid-like and trickled downward.

"What the Hell!" Robert exclaimed. The image on the wall continued to grow. Above what now looked like two black blood dripping handprints, a haggard bloody face began to appear. At first, Robert couldn't tell if the image was a man or a woman as its features weren't recognizable. But then it became much clearer. He could see the hate-filled eyes bulging from sunken skeletal orbs and he knew instantly it was his dead wife Cindy who returned to take her vengeance.

Deep inside his mind, he heard a dying raspy voice crying, "I ... waited ... for ... YOU" repeatedly as it increased in volume with each horrifying repetition. Then the wall seemed to become fluid in nature and the image began to stretch out, coming ever closer to him. He was paralyzed with terror and the horrifying sight before him.

"I'm so ... sorry ... Cindy." Robert began to wail as the wall stretched out toward him, the blackened image reaching for him. Then he felt the icy cold tips of the fingers touch the sides of his face and the inside of his brain screamed with the words, "I ... waited ... for ... YOU!" He felt a stabbing pressure in his chest and pain shooting down his left arm just seconds before he collapsed in a heap onto the apartment floor.

***

The police investigator and EMT stood outside the apartment, discussing what they had found.

God! That smell was unbearable," The police officer said. "How long do you think he was dead?

The EMT thought about it for a few moments and said. "That's hard to say. The medical examiner will have to make that final determination, but to be honest with you, I'd guess it had to be a few weeks, especially based on the decomposed condition of the body."

"Yeah. That was pretty bad. So what do you think?"

"You mean the cause of death?" The EMT said, "Not sure, but my guess would be either a stroke or heart attack. From what the neighbours said, he and his wife only moved into the place a few months ago and apparently she died a few weeks ago. Maybe the stress of losing her was just too much."

The policeman said, "I've heard stories of couples dying within a few days of each other when the surviving spouse can't live without his mate. They often call it dying of a broken heart."

"Well, I don't know about that," The EMT said, "But he definitely died of something. It looked to me like he might have been sitting on the floor looking at that water stain on the wall."

The police officer said, "Could be. I checked with the super and he told me with all the rain we've been having lately, there've been leaks in a number of the apartment units. Apparently, the roof needs to be repaired and the water's leaking down between the walls and has caused the stains."

"Not surprising," The EMT said. "This is an old building. But… did you notice anything unusual … you know … about the stain?"

"No. Not really.,." the police officer said. "It just looks like a big old stain to me."

The EMT said, "you're probably right. But to me, if you look at it a certain way, it resembles the backs of two people's heads walking away. You know … like a man and a woman."

The police officer looked at the image closer, then scratched his head and said, "I don't know … I don't see it. Oh well, I guess with a spot like this, anyone might be able to see just about anything they wanted or needed to see."

"You're probably right," the EMT said. "Well, we'd best be getting the remains out of here."

113

The Dangers of Ill-Prepared
Shellfish (SJ Townend)

Fresh from her scalloped shell she steps, sand between her toes, scaled flesh softening on exposure to the crisp Spring air. Her first day out of the water. So beautiful. Primordial Mermaid; first maiden born of and from the sea. Her Titian hair, all Botticellian waves, cascades down, passing her shoulders, dusting her breasts in thick fronds, curling around her waist. Her flesh becomes less piscine, more pinch-peach-skin soft; it is so as if by magic.

"You're the image of perfection," the four winds whisper into her delicate ears as she tests out her new sleek limbs and glides across the shore. She tilts her head, smiles, uncertain as to what these words mean.

"Perfection?" she asks and inspects the palms and backs of her own hands as if an inquisitive child.

"Be careful not to hurt yourself on the glass-sharp mantle edge of the shell from which you have hatched," the four winds whisper. She smiles, thanks them; her smile is the gift of gratitude.

Her own skin feels divine under her own fingertips. So different to how it had done before, she thinks, although she cannot recall much. She closes her eyes. A smile spreads like sunrise across her porcelain cheeks. She turns back and looks at the sea. *The ocean, it must've been a dream,* she thinks, *my tail is gone and legs have taken its place*. The ocean had certainly been her home up until this moment. She has no memories of what came before and no idea of what is to come.

She stretches out each graceful limb and flexes her spine. With her body liberated from the clam her soft tip-toe gains confidence, develops into a stride, a canter, a skip. Glossy hair whips behind her as she moves with elegance and poise. In and out of the shallow waters she darts, embracing the cool babble and break of waves over new-formed feet.

From further inland, Man, who calls himself Mars, sees this creature of beauty pacing across the shore; this divine thing who does not yet know she is Woman. No longer girl of the sea, no longer mermaid.

He tells her she is perfection, just like the four winds who welcomed her into existence had done and so she trusts him as she had trusted the elements. He steals her from the shore—she, so new, so fresh, is unaware that she has a choice not to go. He makes her his own. She becomes his pride and joy. For a while.

***

Later that week, he dives for and brings her fresh sea pearls, says her beauty outshines even the most polished jewels of the sea. In each pearl she can make out a muffled reflection of her own face. She does not understand his fuss, sees nothing of importance in her own image. He decorates her in nature's gifts, helps her style her hair the way he likes it, purchases and chooses outfits for her to wear.

She thinks she enjoys the attention, she knows no different, for she was raised in a shell by the cold, knife-grey blanket of the sea, her only guidance, intangible, just a few words whispered by the wind.

She knows, because he tells her, that her life with him, in the house, the kitchen, the small fenced-in garden which is not a trap for sun, and the bedroom, is better than anything else she could ever hope for. "I'll provide for you with everything you will ever need," he tells her. And he does. For a while.

He feeds her up on the finest fresh fish, caviar, kisses and caresses the parts of her body she cannot reach alone. He makes her laugh. Sometimes. At first. But often she reaches for her tail and finds it to be still an increasingly distant memory.

***

For the first few years, he brings her flowers on her birth day, which he tells her is the day he found her on the shore. He says it is important to mark the event. Although she cannot recall it, she is certain she existed before this moment, has vague memories of the strange, cramped comfort of a scallop womb, scales where skin now wraps around her bones. But these memories are eaten away

116

around their edges by the passing of time and his persuasion.

He brings generous cloying bunches of lilac sea aster, golden samphire, to mark her birthday each year, tells her their beauty does not compare one touch to hers, tells her she can't have existed before he discovered her and each day she believes a little more in him and a little less in herself.

Each time he brings her flowers, she takes them, thanks him with a bow of her head, a kiss and places them in a vase, the same vase. Always the same vase. This is the vase he tells her she must use. She does not like the vase, but it is the only one. *What choice do I have?* she thinks. He tells her they smell beautiful but she only desires the scent of saline, brine, the marine cloy of her origin.

As the days pass, she watches them wilt, the flowers, long dead already before she had even placed them in the vase in her kitchen. Over morning coffee, she quietly requests that she would like to see where he picked them from, visit— perhaps—the place where the flowers grow wild, at least. She asks him this once—his answer ensures she will never ask the question again, puts to bed her desire to venture away from her home, his house, helps her realise she is lucky he brings her anything at all.

This is, at least, she thinks, *my kitchen, my place of safety, I am blessed to have this humble space,* and she spends time each day watching the flowers decay in a vase she cares not for.

Other than the journey back from the beach many years ago when he brought her home, she has never been anywhere else. *It is at least my kitchen*, she thinks, until he takes that from her as he forces her into a position she never agreed to, pushes himself until no part of the kitchen feels safe to her again.

And as the years pass, her fears and pains ebb and flow. She grows tired of the kitchen. Restless. Each corner is tarnished now with shady memories, shadows and sometimes he makes her bleed.

He continues to bring her flowers on her birth day which is not her true birthday, although she has forgotten who or what she even is. He brings her flowers too, each time he hurts her. He brings her flowers often. Each time, she thanks him, places them in the same vase, watches them wilt, the flowers already long dead.

***

"You are not what you were, my Venus. Your skin has become dry and your hair grey." Mars flares his nostrils, his skin flushes red. He is angered by the smallest of things.

"I'm sorry," she says and pulls up the bed sheet to cover her aging body. She wraps her legs together, pressing her weak frail thighs tight, one atop the other, an ancient thought re-lights her mind's eye: a tail. A caudal fin. A length of overlapping, iridescent scales. Did she once have such a thing?

But her memory is disturbed by violence, bringing her back to the room. She feels the back of his hand against her cheek, the heel of his foot in her long barren womb and then he shouts, pulls back and stops. He leaves the bedroom, slams the door on his way out.

She lies there, numb at first, then burning with pain yet frozen for a while, as tears etch rivulets down her cheeks at right angles to the deep lines the passing of time has used to mark her. Eventually she rises from the prison cell which is her bed and pulls on her smock, each movement pin-balling pain through her bones.

Later in the morning, the stairs play a part in the breaking of our protagonist's leg and Mar's strong arms once more, his overbearing size, play antagonist.

She heals slowly, but never is what she was before and her recovery is marked by more outbursts, more set-backs, as he tells her with his fists how she is becoming less and less perfect with each day that passes. Venus needs a stick now just to move around the house, which has not been a home for a long time, which he gives to her, eventually, in exchange for taking a further fistful of her happiness.

He hides it from her, the stick she needs to walk with, when the food she serves him is substandard. For days she is trapped in a chair in the corner of the kitchen, soiling herself, drowning in a sea of salty tears. *The tears taste better than any kiss he has placed or forced on my lips,* she thinks. She yearns for tart salinity.

Later, he tosses the stick back, only so she can hobble into the small garden to bring in the washing from the line —her spine is curved forwards, one of her legs now skewed in an unnatural alignment, the other managing to just about transport her.

There in the garden, Venus spots a robin, the same robin she often shares a few crumbs with: her only friend. The bird tilts its head at Venus, takes the crumbs, then opens its wonderful wings. *Wings,* she thinks, *such aerodynamic structures, designed to cut through the crisp air absolute.* Oh, to be able to move like fluid. Venus smiles through tears at her avian chum and mouths the word: "Perfection."

One day the bird does not come anymore, has flown away for a final time. She wonders, as she pegs shirts and socks to the line, if the bird is happy. Perhaps her robin has found a better garden. Tilting her head back with elderly caution, she sees a thumb print of swarming birds, a murmuration of starlings up above in the open blue sky and she wonders, she yearns to know, how it feels to glide, to be free.

The night before, Mars had brought war to the dining table, the stew, he had claimed, had been over-cooked, the husk she had baked was too plain. He had placed the bread knife through the palm of her hand. She had held her hand to her chest and the blood had spread, stained the white of her apron red, like a robin's breast. She felt no pain, not now, after all this time. She looked down at the stain forming on her clothes, deaf to his mean, loud words, it merely made her think about her robin. Her robin, who is free to fly away, venture to whenever it wants.

After pegging out the laundry, she hobbles back inside, reclines slowly back into her kitchen chair, looks at her bandaged hand, then her deformed femur, tibia, fibula, arced and now melded, bowing inwards, then curving out like a fish's tail and with her good hand, she pushes back brittle white hair from her face.

Her husband sat in another room. *He will not even notice,* she thinks, *until he requires something to be done.* She takes him a cup of tea, a slice of cake she has baked for no particular reason other than cake is what he had asked her to bake and then she quietly slips on her shoes, drapes a shawl around her hunched shoulders, flaps her wings of stony coloured alpaca wool and, through a hole in the garden fence she pecks with the end of her stick, she leaves.

***

After all these years, she remembers the way. She has played the journey over in her mind many times. Her two feet take her eventually to the beach, which is empty, cold. Rain falls gently. She feels it on her skin, tastes it with her tongue, watches the hazed veil of falling water as, in the distance, it returns to the sea, like she hopes she will too.

121

She sees the giant clam shell, after all these years, it is still there. She remembers it clearly, instantly, as she now also remembers the freedom of her long gone tail. The open maw of the clam beckons her; the four winds encourage each physically arduous step.

She sheds her clothes, strips down until she is as naked as the day she was born and then she tosses her stick into the sea. She steps back inside the place from which she came, she remembers the wilted flowers rotting in the vase. *The vase is his, this shell is mine,* she thinks, *and I, a tired, broken bloom, am ready to wilt.*

Her old body curls forward and she makes herself as small as she can. Near invisible. Unsurprisingly, she does not find this hard. Venus becomes a beautiful grey pearl and around her, the clam lips start to close. *It is as if the shell is smiling, happy to have me back,* she thinks.

For Venus, inside grows darker and she feels squashed, but finally, at long last, she feels safe. "Perfection," she whispers and outside, the four winds echo her final word.

The lips do not close completely though. Both halves of the crimped mantle pause before Venus becomes too cramped inside. A wavy slice of space is left. It is enough for a little light to enter, enough for long strands of her white hair to poke free, to waiver in the gentle sea breeze. It is enough space for her to speak out as and when she pleases. Until the water comes.

She runs her hands up and down her thighs, feeling her skin wrapped loosely like a leathery shawl around her aged bones, knowing her tail will never return, for her time is over. She made her choice, long ago, to switch her tail, to walk bipedal on land.

Water floods in.

The tide pushes forwards and in time, the shell becomes submerged and is carried back out, deeper, into the ocean. Water rushes in through the gap. It fills. Brine fills the shell, fills Venus's lungs, eventually bringing her aged body a certain permanent peace. But the spited spirit of Venus, woman scorned, lives on, haunts the giant clam which now sits at rest, half buried, half exposed, on the sandy blanket of the ocean floor.

***

The sea scallop, giant clam—the strength of its external shell now appears softly feminine, is coated with pink anemones, some sort of coral. *It looks like a pair of beautiful plump lips, the lips of a sweet, young woman,* thinks the pearl diver and finds himself having urges. He pulls down his swimming trunks, grabs the mighty shellfish tightly either side with his neoprene-gloved hands, and, feeling he is out of sight, protected from the eyes of anyone down on the floor of the vast ocean, he places his hard cock in between the undulating bivalve flaps.

But Venus, the very raw ghost of Venus, is vengeful. Venus regrets heavily, eternally, the great sacrifice she made in her hapless quest for love on land. And Venus is hungry.

So finally, she snaps.

Not The Moon (Sandra Stephens)

She is working at her desk when the cramp hits, a poison flower unfolding deep in her belly. She sighs and checks her calendar. Only nineteen days this time. Her cycle is getting shorter.

She has anticipated this and, as before, tried to stave it off. Lots of red meat. Punishing exercise – once running nearly 29 miles at the junior college track, round and round. One by one the walkers and joggers and groups of new mothers pushing strollers came, exercised, and left, until she was circling the darkened track alone, the whisper of her feet and the steady pant of her breath under the watching moon seeming to belong to someone else.

She has even donated blood. None of it works. She has to give in again. And despite her real revulsion at the thought, she feels the old familiar anticipation.

As if on cue, the phone rings. Her intuition, always stronger at this time, tells her she is about to get lucky. Her rising excitement drives the cramps back, snarling, into the dark cave of her vitals and she laughs in relief and excitement.

Fifteen minutes later she is meeting Detective Kelly in the Emergency Room of City Hospital.

"Diana, thanks for getting here so fast. She came in on her own, about three hours ago. Drove herself here right after the attack." Kelly checks his notebook, nods.

He is a stereotypical detective, Diana thinks – tall, dark-haired and square jawed. The only detail that didn't jibe with his Dick Tracy appearance was the color of his eyes – an icy blue that never warmed more than a few degrees, even when he smiled, which was rare.

"Name is Theresa Russell. Thirty-three. He roughed her up pretty good. We got plenty of DNA in the rape kit (a comment that makes Diana's flesh prickle deliciously). We'll run it through the database. Not much in her statement. He hit her from behind – she never got a look at him."

"Where did it happen?" Diana asks.

This is always tricky. It isn't really relevant, but can seem reasonable if asked in just the right way. Detective Kelly, however, has never been a problem. In fact, he is always a virtual fount of information. It took some of the fun out.

"Parking lot of a health club - new place called The Club, behind the Galleria. We'll get the membership list, check it against known offenders. If she's up to it, we'll take her out next week, stake it out, see if she recognizes anyone. SOP."

Diana nods and looks at Kelly with veiled contempt. It didn't seem to bother him that in all the years they'd worked together, he has never caught one of these vicious predators. Like most men, he is content to play at being macho, without offering any real protection or justice to women like Theresa. Or Diana – not that *she* really needed his protection. But to Kelly she says nothing, only smiles a strained smile and looks concerned.

"I'll let you talk to her. I'm gonna make a couple of calls. When I get back we'll talk, I'll collect her personals," Kelly says. He looks at Diana for perhaps a beat too long and the hairs on the back of her neck rise, her upper lip starts to curl. She masks it with a cough.

"Thanks, Detective. I'll do what I can for her."

"Thanks a lot Diana."

She pauses in the act of turning away, her eyes narrowing slightly.

A lot?

In the five years she has known him, Kelly has never wasted words. She searches his face quickly, but sees nothing out of the ordinary. He is a handsome man, manly in a way that she appreciates: athletic build, heavy around the shoulders. Febrile excitement tries to rise, and she coldly crushes it down. Not him, she thinks. Not now. She steps through the curtained partition.

Theresa Russell is a tiny blonde, probably pretty – it is hard to tell, with the battering her features have taken. Her nose is a red and broken pulp. Purplish discoloring around her eyes already darkening to black. Swollen lips, the lower one either split or bitten. She is sleeping the sleep of shock and pain pills, but Diana shrugs. She doesn't need Theresa Russell awake.

She spots what she *does* need on the other side of the bed – a plastic bag. She unworks the knotted top and noses eagerly into the bag. The woman's clothes – the clothes she'd been wearing when she was raped and sodomized – huddle forlornly within.

127

Kelly will pick them up later, for evidence. Diana has never questioned his careless procedure, so preoccupied was she with her own procedures (which were, of course, so much more effective).

Eagerly she pushes her face deeper into the dark mouth of the bag. She closes her eyes, hitches her breath and inhales deeply. Once. Twice. Three, then four times. In this, Kelly had been right – there was plenty of DNA. His and hers. In the pungent secrecy of the bag, Diana grins widely, gums exposed. Her nose tells her what she needs to know: this one is going to be just perfect.

Soon she is pushing through the double glass doors of The Club. Distress at what she is actually *planning* pricks at her, but too late: excitement now has the upper hand. It is always like this after a prolonged abstinence. Her job as counselor at The Women's Center is a job with few benefits - no dental, no health, bad pay, worse ambiance – but it has the great advantage of keeping the periods of abstinence to a minimum. There was a time when it had been worse - - much, much worse.

***

She came into her cycles as a college senior. She'd already known she was different. You can't be the only girl in your high school that doesn't menstruate and *not* know you are different. Even at thirteen, though, she'd understood this wasn't the extent of her difference - - but deeper understanding eluded her then.

At age 14, obeying some awakening instinct, she bought a box of sanitary napkins, threw half of them away, and left the open, depleted box on her bathroom counter. When her mother found the box she hugged Diana and took her to lunch, "Just we two women." She kept the bathroom stocked with sanitary pads (when Diana turned sixteen, the pads were triumphantly replaced with tampons). And each month Diana smuggled the immaculate white pads (and later, the unused tubular missiles) out of the house in her purse, disposing of them in public trash cans.

A bigger difference had been sex. Or, rather, her complete lack of interest in it. This was the real reason for her slow alienation in high school. She didn't flirt or date; she didn't giggle over boys with the other girls. Her cool indifference and her isolation prompted first curiosity, then anger, then rumors. The wilder the rumor, the more they were believed: she took guys on three at a time; she'd been gang-banged by the football team; she was a victim of incest; she was a teenage hooker; she was a lesbian. Because of her sensual beauty, the rumors never accused her of her virginity.

In college the bleeding came. The cramps were agonizing. Her joints and hips filled with a rotten ache, like rusty infected water. Each month was progressively more painful, driving her to lie in bed, rocking in a tight fetal position, only to rise and pace her tiny apartment in the vise of some great restlessness.

129

But her true cycles hadn't begun until the fourth time she menstruated, at the cusp of turning 20. She was a senior. She'd known immediately that she was in the grip of some new thing, some Change.

The first difference was her sudden sexual awakening. From the moment of the first warning cramp – she'd been at the library, studying in the stacks - it felt as though her bloodstream was heating up by slow, hot degrees. Staring blankly at her textbook, sex scenes from movies recurred to her - - they hadn't moved her before, but now she remembered the choreographed sequences of nudity, moaning and thrusting and wet her lips. In fact, she'd become wet all over – her panties clung to her, and she'd broken into a light sweat. Her tongue thickened with lust.

Unable to endure sitting still, she'd checked her books out, studying forgotten, wanting only to walk the night and cool her flushed and burning body. The librarian was a good-looking boy with dark hair, a thin, intelligent face and wire rim glasses. As he scanned her books into the computer, she stared at him mutely, wanting, *needing* to seize him, pull his head to her and kiss him roughly, exploring the dark cave of his mouth with a violent flickering tongue, kiss him, yes, even bite him, and whisper for him to fuck her, *fuck* her, fuck her right now, right here, to take out his cock and *fuck* and *fuck* and...

He felt the weight of her stare. Holding her books out to her, he had tilted his head, smiling.

Anything else you need?"

She'd fled, leaving the books at the counter, frightened but unable to outrun her thoughts. The rituals of bed hadn't soothed her. Teeth brushed, face creamed, Kotex secured - her flow was extraordinarily heavy, she'd been changing every fifteen minutes that day - and still her mind whispered obscenely to her. She lay in her narrow virgin's bed until three-thirty and finally sprang up with a small cry, hands clenched at her sides.

She needed to be outside in the fragrant dark night more than anything, and then she was running, running in her long white nightgown, running down the stairs and through the parking lot, not feeling the broken glass or stones or rough concrete, just running through the soft dark night, running and running, *sprinting* toward some great and looming Change, smelling a thousand fragrances streaming past her, through her, and now she was running in the small copse of trees that separated the apartment complex from the campus, feeling the night run its fingers through her heavy thick hair, tickling her sweating scalp, wanting to laugh up at the overcast sky, wanting to shriek and dance and throw herself down, grinding the points of her hips into the loamy earth and that was when she caught a new scent on the night air. Rich and sweet and salty, it was.....*just what she needed!*

She laughed in savage joy and bounded toward it, and it was the boy from the library, his glasses flashing with moonlight. When he saw her he stopped still, as she did. She stood staring at him, her nightgown blowing gently against her, outlining her legs and breasts and her sweet warm *otherness* now suddenly grown hot and wet. Her nipples stiffened in the quickening breeze; he saw this, eyes darkening, and she felt a fierce heat rush from her groin.

And now she knew what was going to happen – the Change was started, and she was swept by a great hungering lust to *begin*.

She bent low, seized the hem of her nightgown, and in one fluid motion stripped it over her head, tossing it aside. She smelled his confusion and sudden excitement as she stepped towards him, opening her mouth to kiss him. The smell of lust was on his breath, bright purple shot through with red lightning. But there was an undertone of darkness to the smell, wasn't there? Yes, there was - - a blue-black smell of violence, or potential violence, like a hungry animal straining a leash.

They kissed, tongues wrestling urgently. His hands covered her breasts, moving quickly lower even as he bent and took a nipple in his mouth. She spread her legs to give him greater access, clutching his head to her bosom, hips undulating against him.

He lowered her to the ground, and she writhed against him in ecstasy as he worked his jeans open. Arching now, hands tipped with blackening claws, she pressed against him as he suckled her neck and dove up and into her. She screamed her pleasure, the Change accelerating, moving through her now like a grassfire, and hair sprouted to itchingly cover her neck and arms and chest.

He gasped, maybe starting to realize, but it was too late. She bit his tongue deeply, locking her hairy, twisting legs around his buttocks, drilling him deeper into her even as he tried to scream. She rolled him effortlessly onto his back, straddling him for better penetration, and with a final clenching thrust tore his throat out as her orgasm burst through her, lapping frantically at his spouting blood, bathing her snout in it even as his hot semen squirted convulsively into her.

Some time later (minutes? hours?) she woke groggily on his ripped and stiffening carcass. His cock was still buried in her. She leapt nimbly from him (his cock made a small *popping* sound as it freed itself, a cork coming from a bottle) and rolled for a moment in the grass beside the path. She found she could stand with a sort of hunching, bent-legged stance and did, looking about her.

The moon-silvered path glimmered at her. Her nightgown billowed gently toward her. She slipped it on and ran back to her apartment, the Change reversing even as she went. By the time she locked herself in her apartment, she could stand wholly upright, her limbs once again straight and slender. By the time she had showered the dirt and blood and pieces of torn flesh from her body, her fangs and claws had fully retracted. And when she crawled into bed, the only evidence that she was something other than the Diana who had slept in this bed every night of the past four dry, sterile years was a downing of black hair lightly furring her arms and legs. When she woke, even that was gone.

But, there was also this: her period was over, finished, the heavy flow completely dried up, the rotten aching of her joints replaced with an oily, limber smoothness.

She was never suspected. It never occurred to anyone to suspect a human – much less a girl whose flawless white skin, delicate features and long-lashed eyes prompted nothing darker than a lust-touched awe and envy in those who knew her. When the mutilated and partially eaten body was found, campus police warned of wild dogs, set traps and instituted a curfew.

The guilt came after. Although the memory slowly dissipated as she moved deeper into the safe days of her cycle, she never forgot, not really. She lost the details but retained a clear imprint of the overwhelming excitement, the lust, that had consumed her as she Changed. She was revolted and horrified and yet some sneaking, skulking part of her longed to repeat it, looked forward to the time when she could, and would, do it again.

No Gypsies needed here to tell her what she was, and why. She simply was. The knowledge was a well, suddenly fountaining to life deep inside of her. She understood that her kind had always been women, and that the Change had never been brought on by the moon but by the relentless, cycling power within her own body. She instinctively knew there must have been others before her- after all, one of the first slang terms for menstruation that a girl learns is The Curse.

134

In all of these years, she had never seen or smelled or sensed Another.

The guilt had slowly been replaced by fear, as she came to understand her predicament. This was a small college town. One or two more savaged corpses would create a panic - - and, eventually, a search party. She remembered waking on the corpse – how long had she slept in her satiety? Long enough (*pop!*) for rigor to set in – long enough for a search party with dogs and guns to make short work of her.

When subsequent Cycles began, she grimly set about damping down the devouring, needful lust. Cold showers. Running. Driving. But now came a frightening realization; almost anything stimulated her during this time, beckoning her dark desires. She learned to avoid movies – the sex excited her to an unbearable frenzy. Public gatherings were agony - - the sound of blood rushing below rich sweet-salt flesh deafened her, made it impossible to speak without drooling.

She'd been horrified to find that masturbation brought on the Change. She had tried the experiment on a Friday, and spent the weekend pacing her apartment, half-fanged and hairy, nearly mad with pain and frustration and fear. But with each unconsummated cycle, her periods became heavier and more painful, nearly debilitating in their force. The time between them became shorter and shorter, until she was continuously bleeding – a viscous brackish red-black flow that saturated her sanitary pads in minutes (tampons were a thing of

135

the past, triggering the Change even faster than masturbation). Her constantly aching joints reduced her normal fluid stride to a kind of limping hobble.

She both dreaded and needed the Change. A kill stretched her cycle to twenty-eight or thirty days (eventually she'd come to think of her period as the times in between the bleeding, and not the blood itself). Two kills within a cycle staved off menstruation for forty to fifty days. She had never killed more than twice during a cycle, for the simple reason that it was risky. If she killed too often within a radius of time and miles, she might become a suspect.

She knew that she could easily lengthen her cycles to annual affairs, or longer – the price would be carnage, and she would almost certainly be hunted, or even killed outright. But after three or four cycles without a kill, twisting in her bed with unrequited pain and desire, the idea would beckon her. One way or another, it would bring sweet release.

After graduating she moved to a large city and held a variety of night jobs. Night jobs gave her a reason to stalk the darkest part of the city in the darkest part of the night, her kills safely piled on the charnel heap of unsolved murders common to big cities.

The Women's Center had been her fifth such job, and suddenly, miraculously, the hateful dawn raids of the drunk and homeless were a thing of the past. She had a new hunting ground now, in the endless stream of victims that came to the Center.

To Diana, they all had the same yellow-brown smells of pain and fear, depression and defeat.

And during the start of her cycle, when her senses sharpened to an almost unbearable keenness, their skin and hair and clothing smelled sharply of the men that had abused them.

Just like Theresa Russell.

***

Now, at The Club, the revulsion is receding, replaced by the high excitement of lust singing in her veins. She stands in the center of the room, a collage of richly textured scents swirling around her head. She picks up the scent of the rapist almost immediately: thin and acrid, it smells of sour milk with an undertone of cheap tobacco. And something else - something nasty and hot, barely suppressed. Something like pus bubbling beneath an old scab.

She works her way through the easier exercises (but no heavy exertion; in her state it could bring on the Change in a surge of testosterone-powered strength, sending the club members screaming into the night like frightened hyenas). While she works out, she idly reads the posters that decorate the club walls. Most are devoted to the marshmallowy before and buff-after body improvement theme. All have the same assertion/command in blood red letters across the bottom: IF YOU DON'T LIKE YOUR BODY, CHANGE.

Amen to that, she thinks. She couples with the shiny weight machines until the yellow-green smell

137

of the rapist clogs her sinuses and slicks her body with expectation.

As his workout ends, his sweat-fed scent darkens into olive tones. She manages to exit the club just ahead of him, swinging her hair conspicuously, and now his scent changes, brightening dangerously – it is the electric greenish gray of a forest waiting for a storm.

She digs in her purse as she walks, keeping her head low and hunching her shoulders slightly forward. She stumbles into a dark alley, and now his scent deepens even as his step quickens - a murky green swirling with flashes of brooding ochre.

Halfway down the long alley, she stops at the lone car that isn't hers, still rooting in the purse, making soft, frustrated sibilants and plosives.

He says "Hey" and she turns, the tusklike fangs already beginning to push against the curve of her upper lip, and his scent is black and red lightning bolts when his fist crashes into her eye. She falls, clutching her face with both hands and then he is on her, not noticing that she doesn't scream, already yanking her sweat pants down (she'd left off her panties, even then anticipating the ease of elastic sliding smoothly over naked hips) and ramming himself into her as he grasps her hands to pinion them over her head. Diana also thrusts - - thrusts her hips to meet the sword of his cock, and thrusts her hairy, elongating, snarling face into his own shocked visage. She hooks her lower fangs through his lips and screams "HEY!" into his face, which is going through a Change of its own as he realizes just who the wolf REALLY is around here.

She keeps screaming it with each thrust, liking it: "HEY! HEY! HEY!", drowning out his screams until even her vocal chords Change and she can only growl and snarl and bark (and even the barks sound like "Hey!") and slaver and drool until she is finished.

In the shadows, Detective Kelly smokes and watches. When the feeding begins, he slips away and returns to his cruiser, hidden two blocks up. As always, he is glad to put distance between himself and Diana. He doesn't want to be the one to find out that her focus can extend beyond her victim when she is....in *flagrante delicto*.

He smiles at the thought, and his hands tremble only a little as he starts his cruiser and points north. When he has put a safe amount of distance between himself and the alley he calls the Dispatcher, who responds immediately to the real tension and excitement in his voice. At least he doesn't have to act.

"Officer needs assistance. Shots fired at 76th and Carlisle. Repeat, shots fired at 76th and Carlisle." This was a crack playground, about two miles from The Club. Kelly is only a few blocks from the spot as he speaks.

"Repeat, officer needs assistance. Request back-up immediately."

He doesn't really listen as the Dispatcher squawks excitedly back. He thinks of Diana. By now she will be coming to, still crouched over the rapist. She'll have plenty of time to get home and clean up before he returns to the area to retrieve the body. He will wrap it in the stiff plastic sheeting in his trunk and bury it at an abandoned gravel quarry south of the city, where at least two other corpses were already interred.

He reseats the police radio and turns on his siren. As he drives, he sings under his breath.

"And another one down and another one down, another one bites the dust!" An oldie but a goody, as his partner (who has also bitten the dust) used to say. Kelly giggles.

Since Diana has moved to the city there has been a significant reduction in the incidence of rapes and murders on his beat, which of course he can take credit for, which of course he fully intends to do in the fall when he begins the campaign for Police Chief. If the outcome looks in doubt, he will simply stop burying the bodies. Given the.... *thoroughness*....of Diana's work, it will only take two or three discoveries to spin the city into panic. In the grip of panic, the voters will gladly turn to the fearless lawman who eliminates the beast among them. Who knew how far he could go?

Politics certainly make strange bedfellows, Kelly thinks. Another oldie but goody. He giggles again. He is still humming when he screeches to a stop at 76th and Carlisle, scattering the punks like a pack of hyenas before the righteous white eye of his spotlight.

Cocooned (Rie Sheridan Rose)

When I first saw her on the dark street, she was shivering, hopping from one bare foot to the other as the slush turned her flesh blue. She stopped me as I went by, clutching the tail of my cloak and beseeching me with every fiber of her being, "Please, guvnor, buy me matches? Me da said not to come home with a single box."

She couldn't have been more than ten.

I looked into her tray. More than a dozen crude boxes scattered in the bottom. It would take her hours more to sell them in this world where most hurried by without seeing the girl behind the rags and tangles. But there was beauty in that delicate face. It called for me to shelter and protect it—as only I could.

"I'll take all your matches, if you will carry them home for me."

She pulled herself up and stepped back, "And what would you be expecting for that service?"

Intelligence, too. What an intriguing child.

"Nothing, my dear. Companionship at dinner, perhaps?"

I had her attention now—it was clear in the quiver of her lip as her teeth grazed it. The quickening of her pulse at her throat. The compulsive way she straightened and re-straightened the boxes of matches.

"I got to be home before midnight, or he'll lock the door and make me sleep in the street."

"I'll see you there." I held out my hand and fought to keep from trembling lest she didn't take it.

With one last glance around the darkened street corner, she put her hand in mine. I heaved a silent sigh of relief and started homeward. I'd been alone for so long….

By the end of the second block, she seemed to come to the decision she could trust me and began to chatter like a magpie.

"My name's Annie McLean. What's your name?"

I vowed not to lie to this child. Whatever the cost. "My name's Marcellus Lecante, though I am Mark to most of my acquaintances."

"Do you have a family? Me mum died last summer. Da ain't me real father. Mum married him to put a roof o'er our heads and then she died and left me there."

"I'm sure she didn't intend to." I fought to hide my smile.

"Mebbe not, but it don't make it no better. Do you know how to read?"

The question took me by surprise. "Yes."

She stopped dead in her tracks. "You do?" she breathed. "Could you teach me?" She leaned toward me, hands clasped before her chest, matches spilling unheeded to the snow.

"Yes, of course," I promised recklessly.

She took my hand again, skipping through the slush now, heedless of the cold biting her toes. "I've always dreamed of reading.... Mum knew a few bits and said she'd teach me when I was twelve, but then the coughing sickness took her early. Da don't believe in such foolishness. As long as he can make his mark, he considers he's got enough learning."

"How old are you, Annie?"

"Ten and a half."

So young...so vulnerable.

I don't know what had possessed me to invite her home. Yes, I was lonely, but could she be the companion I needed so desperately? A child, and so innocent of life?

On the other hand, what we could learn together....

We arrived at my building and climbed the stair to my flat. Annie's mouth hung open as she felt the carpeting between her toes and stared at the opulent wallpaper of the hallway.

"Cor...are you a lord?"

"No, just well-off. Come, sit by the fire. I'll make you some hot chocolate." I stirred the coals to life and added fuel. Soon the flames flickered merrily and Annie had curled her feet under her skirts to thaw.

She accepted a mug of thick chocolate gratefully. She took a tentative sip and her eyes widened. "A little taste of heaven, that."

"Annie...would you like to stay here with me? I would teach you to read and to be a lady and anything else you might want me to teach you."

Her eyes narrowed. "What would you want in return? I'm a good girl, for all Da's trying."

My heart clenched at the thought. "I ask nothing from you, my dear. Just to keep me company."

The calculation on her face was decades older than she was. Unless I intervened, Annie was well on her way to a life unloved with a passel of brats clinging to her skirts and death before thirty.

"If I say yes, will you be my new Da?"

"In a manner of speaking."

She sipped at her chocolate in silence. I could almost see the thoughts running through her head. Her eyes moved restlessly as she weighed her options.

Finally, she sighed and set aside the cup on the side table.

"I ain't had much of a life anyway. So, I suppose whatever you have in mind is better than home."

"I swear to you, Annie. I'm not proposing anything untoward. Let me ask you a question...how old do you think I am?"

She cocked her head. "You look about as old as Mum when she died...so twenty-five or so?"

"What would you say if I told you I was more than two thousand years old?"

"I'd say you were a right liar and I'll be on my way, thank you very much."

"No, really, I mean it. I've seen whole civilizations rise and fall. And you could too."

She had pushed herself into the corner of the chair, cowering like a frightened mouse. "It's touched in the head you are, then?"

I hunkered down before the chair. "No, my dear, I promise." I held out a hand to her. "We've been inside by the fire for some time now. Touch my hand."

Tentatively, she reached forward. "Why, you're cold as ice, sir!"

"One of the consequences of my existence, I fear."

"What are you?"

Perceptive. The right question to ask.

"That's a hard question to answer, Annie. Have you ever seen a caterpillar in its cocoon, preparing to emerge as a butterfly?"

"Not in the East End," she answered dryly, again showing herself to be wise beyond her years.

"I'll show you one day…. A caterpillar spins itself into a hard shell and sleeps inside as its body changes to become a beautiful, flying butterfly. I shed my human skin to become something else. I offer you the same gift. To become something new and different. Ageless and beautiful."

"How?"

"Come with me." I gave her my hand and led her towards the bed chamber.

She pulled back. "You said—"

"Don't worry, Annie. This is where I keep the cocoon." I opened the door and pointed to the coffin in its place on the bed. "We'll sleep inside the box during the day and emerge at night as beautiful, ethereal creatures."

"Will it hurt?"

"Only a very little."

145

It was shortly before I usually retired, but not much. "Come."

I walked to the coffin and threw back the lid. Climbing inside, I held out my arms, and Annie tentatively crossed the room.

She stepped into the box beside me, easing herself down into the satin cushions. "What must I do?" she whispered.

"I'll bite my wrist and you must drink of my blood while I do the same from yours. This will bind us together. When we wake tomorrow at dusk, you'll be transformed and your lessons will begin."

Eyes shining with hope and trust, she held out her wrist.

Now she's sleeping the sleep of transformation, cradled in my arms.

I'm too excited to sleep…. At last I will have a companion. And I will keep her safe.

Cocooned.

My Body is My Own (SJ Townend)

Mr Brownstone appeared at the front of the queue of twelve-year-old kids stretched round the outside of the gymnasium and hollored, "Prantler. James Prantler."

James gulped. The nervous, dimpled smile he'd been masquerading with slipped, wet clay, down his face, as his tired, green eyes widened. "Shit," he mouthed to the boy behind. James shuffled forwards, heart in throat, and followed Brownstone through.

Inside, Brownstone, Head of Mathematics, took a close-range photograph of James's eye, helped him press his fingertips, one by one, onto the screen of a tablet, and then directed him to a chair where James sat down, belly of nerves. Mademoiselle Lavigne, French department, whipped out the clippers and cleared a square inch of hair from behind his ear. The ice-cold gel she smeared onto his exposed scalp smelt stringent, threatening, like his stepfather's vodka-laced breath.

The third adult in the room—a lady with medi-gloved hands who James didn't recognise—tore open a pouch and pulled from it a small, black device no larger than a hair pin. She pushed it against James's sticky skull.

The lady nodded at Brownstone, who, in response, tapped his tablet screen. "Little scratch," she said and stepped back. James, eyes squeezed closed, fists clenched like buns, for the first time in his life, wished for the air quality alarm to ring.

Without human touch, the device beeped and pierced into James's skull. He internalised a scream as pain pin-balled from under his ear to the space behind his eyes, chased by extreme coldness.

"You might experience 'iced-spaghetti-head' for a moment," the lady said, her dirtied medi-gloves already discarded.

James grappled at his temples. Brownstone batted his feverish hands away. "No touching."

"It's killing me."

"Please, don't touch the neuroprosthesis—its silk nanotubules are corkscrewing through your prefrontal cortex. Should settle soon," the lady said, her hands in clean gloves in preparation for the next child, "although you may experience tingling next week, as the brain-machine interface calibrates. It needs to harvest data on your basal-wave levels and your pheromone receptors, to align them with the Conception Prevention Conditioning Database."

She went on to defend EarthGov's CPC Campaign: "...and sterilisation at birth, too expensive. Also, inhumane..."

Technical words billowed like smoke, but James had stopped listening. He was twelve, had no idea what she was on about; was just glad the pain had started to ease.

Momentarily, they allowed him to recuperate while they sanitised equipment, then Brownstone left to escort through the next child, and Bambi-legged James, his hands balling and flexing with discomfort, was dispatched through another exit. "Head straight to Programming - over in F-block - follow the temporary signs."

***

Not a day passed when James didn't think about ripping the device from his scalp. Puberty? Horrendous. Monstrous changes: body odour, acne, inappropriate stiffenings, even his sweet angelic voice which he could wrap his mother around his finger with had been taken. He wanted to chat with cute girls, hug them, maybe kiss one. This was all off-limits now.

It itched. Bald patch, aged fifteen. He'd scratched at the damn chip so hard, hair behind his ear had fallen out and refused to return. *At least I can still touch myself,* he thought, tucked up under his duvet in the corner of his bedroom. He zoomed in on Samantha's Insta photo on his smart-screen. *She's perfect.*

What he wouldn't do to share a kiss, a consensual touch with her. Half the school fancied her; even Brownstone lingered near her desk a little longer than necessary. Brownstone: late fifties, 'Breath of Death', born the year before the inaugural Black Box Programme, probably the only person in school enjoying the campaign.

***

At the beginning, before they'd all witnessed

149

the extent of the implant's control, Samantha would walk around giggling, a circle of plainer girls shielding her, creating the necessary distance buffer between Samantha's body and hordes of horny kids. But some of those horny kids still tried to get closer—despite verbals from staff—and their hacked sensory neurones detected her pheromones, triggering their rewired arousal circuitry. Electric shocks ensued. They learned hard and fast proximity wasn't worth the consequences, the humiliation.

But Rick Redfield tolerated the shocks. He thought he'd cracked it, only to discover the Eroticism Signal, which put a stop to further tomfoolery. He got so close to Samantha, an alarm began, emitted from peripheral high-mounted speaker arrays: a sharp arc of sound, a war-siren that made a reedy whisper of the air quality alarm by comparison.

Class mates pointed and jeered: 'perv', 'sex-pest'. Cheeks flushed crimson. Once they'd learnt about the ES sirens, the majority of the kids started to give Samantha, and anyone else they were sweet on, plenty of distance.

There were scraps every day on the fields: tumbling balls of frustrated kids definitely *not* attracted to each other pounding each other, gut and jaw, pulling each other's hair. The staff became well versed in fight-dispersal protocol.

But, worst of all—the home DM'ing. Straight to mum/dad/carer:

<u>WARNING.</u>
YOUR CHILD APPROACHED ANOTHER AND BECAME SEXUALLY AROUSED.

Rapid conditioning ensued—because to sit across the dinner table from a parent who knew you'd had an erection, a wide-on, a hardening of your nipples, whatever, at school that day was The Worst.

*

E-MAIL: @ALL_PARENTS
FLESH CRIME: 10.48am - 25th June 2093 - School Field
Mark Reeves (16)
Gina Blaystock (16)

***

Gina and Mark, behind the bike sheds, wanted to feel the press of lips, couldn't resist the temptation of skin against bare skin. The sirens played a new ear-piercing wail on June 25th. The pair shot out from their love-nest, pulling down raised shirts, zipping up flies, tightening belts. The entire school witnessed the aftermath of their Flesh Crime.

Two Securidrones descended from resting nooks, lowered their robotic arms, hissing as aluminium syringe-tipped knuckles shuffled and shook, and injected them both with needlefuls of neon fluid. Both kids dropped, stones down a well.

Silence rippled across the playground. Heads

turned. The automatic 8-foot gate cranked open and an e-van, similar in shape to the fossil-fuelled hearses of the past, which they knew from History had been used to chauffeur coffins, pulled up near the slumped pile of failed Romeo and Juliet. Pupils watched in horror, slack-jawed, as encircling teachers lifted the deadweights into the vehicle.

***

"It'll get easier," James heard his mother muttering as he slunk down the stairs to join his mother and stepfather, Noel, for dinner. "He'll control the urges, until he's passed financial threshold and the health test on his thirtieth. The government'll deem him worthy for nuptials, won't they?"

"Stupid little tosser," said Noel, catching James's eye, slipping a sardonic grin to his 15-year-old stepson. James glowered back.

On pulling out his chair, James let its legs scrape across the floor; tension as thick as the tofu slab on his plate. *God, I want to deck him. Mess him up good,* thought James.

Noel, with narrowed eyes, stared back hard at James's contorted face, then wrapped his arms around his wife's shoulder and squeezed her playfully on the breast.

"Wahey!" said Noel, not taking his eyes off James.

"Hands off, you cheeky ape!"

James looked away, disgust curling in his

152

stomach, as, across the table, his mother kissed Noel passionately. James picked up his cutlery, the steak knife glinting under the daylight simulation panel, and sliced, sliced, into his veggie t-bone. He ate rapidly, silently, wanting to escape the table as fast as possible.

On finishing, he wiped the serrated blade and, not entirely sure why, slid it up his sleeve to take to his room.

***

"You okay?" James squinted and edged as close as he knew he safely could; still just a little too far to see if she was laughing or crying.

"It's not fair." *Definitely crying.* As Samantha, slumped in the sunshine against the wall of the science block, spoke, he heard sadness resonate in her voice. "Even Maria won't sit by me anymore. DM'd me last night, said she's got feelings for me too now."

"Sorry to hear that." James pushed his hands down hard into his pockets, prayed he was far enough from her his implant wouldn't detect her scent. "Wish I could come over there, for a hug, you know, as friends."

"She's my best friend—was. It's too much, you know?" she lifted her head, mascara spider-webbed down her cheeks. "We're compassionate, sentient beings, fucksake. We should be able to choose what we do with our own bodies, have autonomy over them."

153

"Need a tissue?" Unsure what some of the words she'd used meant, he reached for the packet of Kleenex in his pocket. "Mum says it stings when make-up gets in her eyes."

"Never wearing make-up again." She shook her head, pulled a tissue from her own sleeve and, with fury, began scrubbing. "Hate my face. Want to rip it off." Mauling her cheeks with her fingernails, thin lines of red sprung up.

"But you're—" he started and couldn't finish, nerves getting the better. She scowled.

"Hate my face, my hair, my tits—everything. Despise it all. I just want someone to be able to hold me, to love me that way, you know, no strings. It's no fun doing it alone, is it?

"Well, I'm not sure I fully agree there . . . self-servicing is still *quite* fun," he replied, arching a brow. The corners of her lips tipped upwards.

That smile. Why does she have to be so damn perfect? He took a step back, as he'd become conditioned to do when someone attractive approached.

"Yeah, I guess." She sniffed, blew her nose. Even through charcoal panda bear smudges, her wet eyes sparkled. "It's not our fault though, is it? None of this is; too many people, babies. Why are we being punished?"

She scrunched her tissue up her sleeve and thrust her hair apart to reveal the sore patch where her 'Hitler Box' had been inserted. He shrugged, lifted his own hand, fiddled with the mess on the side of his own head. Her metallic scalp tag glinted

154

and reminded James of what he'd got in the side pocket of his cargo trousers.

"I mean, if you're desperate, if we ever, you know, get past this, I'd be more than happy to hug you and stuff. As friends." He blushed. All the nights he'd spent jacking off to her image—*thank heck these boxes don't allow complete telepathy*, he thought, *things could be a LOT worse.*

She slipped him a flirtatious grin. "That'd be nice. And if I liked the way you smelt, if we were, you know, compatible, maybe we could take things further?"

Christ alive, he could feel himself stiffening. In his head, red flags were waving, alarm bells ringing. If he wasn't careful, real bells would ring soon too. With fingers, he pegged his nose, and took another Neil-Armstrong-sized step back. He couldn't face Noel with an Eroticism email. He'd rather die. At least thinking about his stepfather put heed to the semi brewing in his underwear.

"I'm clinically depressed," she said. "They put me on tablets. 'Mood-levellers'. Bastard buzz-kill pills. Don't even work. Can't even orgasm on them—don't even feel like trying. I just want to be held." She started crying again.

"Woah." His skin flushed.

"Sorry, too much info?" through her tears, she snorted, chuckled.

At least she's laughing now, he thought, *but, dammit, even her laughter is sexy.*

James reached further into his pockets, felt the odd comfort of the knife: warm, glass-sharp under

155

his thumb pad—fantasies of stabbing his six-foot-three stepdad in the thigh would probably remain just that, fantasies.

"What's in your pocket? Pleased to see me?" she gestured at his trouser leg. Looking down, it had given him a bit of a bulge.

"Ah, shit...this? No...no, God no. I mean yes—you're beautiful—but no...it's a knife."

"A fucking what? A knife?" she stood up. He stepped back, the distance-tango. "Great idea," she said. Her eyes shone, a spark of madness to them, like the knife had conveyed the night before.

"What do you mean—'great idea?'"

"I could sheer off my hair. Stop wearing makeup. Dress like a dork. If I'm unattractive, I can be around friends again . . . squeeze in the occasional hug . . . get invited to sleepovers."

She smiled again, this time wide-eyed. *Terrible idea,* he thought, but realised it'd given her hope, made her feel better, plus, he'd never get to actually touch her anyway, he'd manage with her Insta photo, Mrs. Palm-ula Handerson, party-for-one. *What harm is there in helping—I could be her knight in armour, a friend.*

He pulled out the knife and shoved it across the dirt. "All yours. Hope it works—though I do find girls with shaved heads super-hot," *dang my honest-when-nervous tongue.* He let his gaze fall to the floor, rammed his hands back in his pockets, kicked a pebble.

Samantha picked up the blade and parted her hair above her right ear. That's when he realised—

she had no intention of cutting her hair, she wanted to carve out her implant.

"Stop! No, Samantha! The probe's two inches deep in your skull, the sensors stretch throughout your entire cortex, if you dig it out, you'll fit, bleed to death."

Samantha, eyes and ears closed for business, dug the tip of the blade in. A trickle of blood snaked around her ear, followed by a small gush. He watched, panicking, as she drove the blade in deeper. He couldn't bare it. Despite the dread of his parents finding out he'd smelt a girl, had had sexual thoughts, despite the fact Noel would ridicule him for months, years even, if an Eroticism email was sent home, he couldn't let her mutilate herself. The girl could die.

James dashed forwards, sharp zaps progressing to a cranking siren in his skull as he approached her. *Too close.* The Eroticism Siren burst down his auditory nerve, screamed through the speakers strung up around the school perimeter. So loud, his molars hummed. Lunging towards her, towards the steel blade as blood spat out from her skull, he knocked it from her hand.

"The heck you do that for? Want. This. Bastard. Out," she yelled, reaching for it. He blocked her reach, his hand brushing against her cheek as he did, *so close, flesh close,* and then, for James, time stood still.

The sensation: unmatchable.

Her skin: so *fucking* soft.

Despite her warm blood on his hand, her skin

157

had felt like nothing he'd ever touched before. Close enough to smell her, to inhale the invisible biochemicals seeping from her pores, flooding the air, elation and horror quiksilvered through his veins. She smelt of nothing, a little coppery maybe, blood, but his implant detected thirty-nine different semiochemicals, each one widening blood vessels, sharpening senses, preparing his body for sexual encounter.

Overly sensitized perhaps, after years of touch-repression, he'd never felt so turned on and so afraid in his whole fifteen years.

Pulling back, he kicked the knife into the ditch behind Science, but it was too late. Not for her, Samantha was fine. With her weathered tissue, she dabbed at the wound she'd made, the bleeding easing. But for James: too late.

The Eroticism Siren changed. He'd touched her. Receptors in his skin awakened, molecules of Samantha's biofragrance seeped through his epidermis, travelled in his blood, up to the unit in his brain.

The Securidrone's 'Flesh Crime' tone filled the air.

"Shit," she screamed, "behind you—run!"

Too late. He froze, statue-boy, overwhelmed by the sight. Robotic arms, shuffling knuckles carrying myriad needles of neon fluid jabbed at his cheek, neck, flesh of his lower arm. Like a racehorse brought down at an impossible fence, he pooled to the ground.

Kids flocked from everywhere. In front of the

158

entire school, Samantha wept as, bundled in the e-van, James's motionless body was driven away.

***

Seven years of obsessive research and academia; that was how the following years panned for Samantha. After acing her bioengineering degree, specialising in black box technology, she earned a place across the country to study her Masters. She snapped up the offer—a clean break from hometown hell. But as soon as she relocated, she realised it didn't matter where she resided—people still wouldn't come near her.

She'd never gotten used to the lack of touch, despised the isolation, yet hadn't become desperate enough to stoop to one of the downtown 'feeler shops' where elderly, implant-free people—largely men—charged for 'hugs, massage, more'. Instead, she studied. Hard. She'd set her heart on finding a way to override her box, felt it was a basic human right. She wanted answers, *needed* rid of the bastard metal thorn in her skull, because more than anything, Samantha craved to be held by someone she cared for in that way.

***

Dr. Zee-Wang walked on stage for his lecture: *Advances in Neurohack Software.* She'd seen him in the cafeteria: a little taller than her, a great deal smarter. They'd chatted over coffee from opposite

ends of a table, and he'd invited her to the extra-
curricular lecture. She'd eagerly accepted;
somehow, she'd learn: how to mute it, destroy it.
Maybe at some point she'd even get that hug. If not,
she'd gain employment in the industry, earn enough
to apply for 'conjugational rights', and in another
seven years, get the damn thing switched off.

As Zee-Wang's laser beam tip started to dance
over the lecture screen, she looked around the near-
empty theatre.

Shit!

Even from the across the large room, she
recognised his dimple, his ocean-green eyes.

Can't be, can it?

She crabbed along the row, crept back up the
aisle, found an empty seat, a little closer, behind
him, in order to confirm.

It is!

It was him.

But surely—he's dead, I saw him die!

James, the kid who'd risked his life to save
hers, was there, under the same roof, alive.
Somehow they'd both ended up at the same
university, same department, maybe even studying
on the same Program.

***

After the lecture, she stealthily followed James
to the university library where she hid and watched
him as he studied. She mulled over all the questions
she wanted to ask, how she'd thank him for what he

160

did.

Evening beckoned. James, owl-eyed tired but seemingly eager to let off some steam, left the library and headed to the pub. Inconspicuously, she wound herself around lampposts, ducked in and out of shadows, behind him.

Inside, she watched him as he fist-bumped the bartender, hugged friends, danced haphazardly to some sort of nu-metal. From afar, Samantha saw it all. How she longed for human contact, freedom of body; what she wouldn't do.

A double whisky inside of her, three of those, Dutch courage, from her shaded corner, she observed. *I'll approach him, soon. I need answers. Hell, I've got to thank him,* she thought and hours later, James left alone, with the shadow of Samantha in his wake.

"James," she called out from under the orange blush swell of a streetlamp, "James, is it really you?" He spun round, rubbed his eyes. *He doesn't recognise me,* she thought, heart knocking in her throat.

"Samantha?"

She nodded, hesitated. He held up his hand. Not to stop her, but to beckon. "It's fine," he said, his face a picture of shock. "Come as close as you like, you can't hurt me." He tapped his temple. "Mine's switched off."

"Off? What— How— I don't understand. I...thought you were dead?" She moved closer, to try to study his scar. A zap of pain flickered through her skull. She winced. Too close. *Dammit!* She'd gotten close enough to smell the ale on his breath, top notes of something else, an invisible tang, which invited her closer. She wanted to inhale more . . . then she twigged: pheromones.

James, brows hoisted, watched her spasm and writhe like one of those toys that dance when you push its base as a shock zagged through her brain. He sensed her pain, his face softening. He laughed his sweet laugh. "Maybe *you* should stay back?"

At school, she hadn't been attracted to him— not goofy James Prantler, some kid in the year below—but years had passed. Now, James was a brave, kind man with a sweet, dimpled smile. She inhaled deeply, moved inwards, her commonsense displaced by the buzz of alcohol and mood pills. Another zap. She pinched the bridge of her nose, gritted her teeth. "Fucksake." She tried to push through the discomfort, but the zaps intensified. She stopped, spoke: "I want to thank you."

"Thank you," said James ruefully. "And no, I'm not dead."

"W...what happened to you?"

She watched him weigh his words before speaking. "Walk with me," he said with a tilt of his head.

He told her about the neon sedation, the surgery, his relocation, how he'd been used as a deterrent.

***

"So they took it all? Didn't just give you The

162

Snip?"

"Smoother than a Ken doll down there." He winked, wiped a tear with the back of his hand, then smiled. "They left me a hole. For urination."

"Christ," she replied, sobered by his story and the cold night air. They strolled, saying nothing, both trying to process the chance encounter, the things they'd talked about, until Samantha broke the silence. "It's disgusting, what they're doing, controlling us, dictating what we do with our bodies." She stopped, placed her hands on her hips and looked him straight in the eye. "Aren't you depressed? Don't you get...urges?"

"Honestly? I'm okay, in a way. At the moment. And no, no urges, not like that. I've things I enjoy: friends, music, research. Life goes on, you know. Kids, sex? They're not everything."

"U-huh."

"Plus," he hesitated, drew a breath, "they told me I made it through round one. I've progressed to 'stage two'. They put something into my jaw which extends into my ears." He lifted his top lip. Samantha gasped. Four of his molars had been pulled, replaced with glassy spikes, serrated shark's teeth, each with a blue-neon light glowing, throbbing, within.

"The fuck," she recoiled, "is that?"

"Neo-diamond. No idea. They said I'll find out when it's switched on. I can't for the life of me pull it out—it's bonded to my jawbone."

***

163

A curl of a breeze brought up a waft of his natural scent. *So good.* She inhaled, her head spinning, and made a decision, a choice: brushing the back of her hand against his bare arm, she asked: "Hold me."

"Samantha— "

More zaps. The Flesh Crime Siren squealed inside her skull, then blasted from speakers along the side of the path. She shoved her fingers in her ears to no avail.

"I want it out. Don't care—I'd never bring kids into this shit-show world anyway. I want free of this fucking box," she shouted. "May I?"

James nodded. "If you're sure— "

She straightened her spine, stepped forwards, and wrapped her arms around him. Then, she kissed his cheek.

Brain zaps. Cacophonous noise.

Pulling back, heart and head thrumming, a strong smile spread on her face. She shouted above the siren: "I'll find you, James, when it's done . . . I'm going Trojan . . . and once they've given me back my freedom, I'm taking these bastards down from within."

From its metal nest atop a streetlamp, a Securidrone descended. Samantha stood stock-still. Ominous knuckles of metal unfurled. Needle-nails injected her with neon.

James caught her as she collapsed, his heart pounding. With shaking hands, he laid her on the path as gently as he could and pulled off his top.

After caressing her hair from her pale face, he lifted and placed her head on his balled shirt. Menacing sirens growing ever nearer, he stayed with her, hoping it would not be the last time he saw her, until he was sure he could see the electric van approaching. Then, with his veins reflooding with the old fear he had tried to forget, had stashed deep for so long, and a speed, a new speed, that he had not known he possessed, and a stellar pulse of blue light emitting from his jaw, like lightning, he ran.

Souls To Take (Olivia Arieti)

Leopold had reached the utmost of evil and was no longer aware of how deep he had sunk into the hellish pit. He had been perverse since a child, since he stole his little sister's rag dolls and cut them up or drowned them in the tub. The pleasure of seeing them get more and more swollen, their eyes glaring at him as if really animated, was incommensurable. Cruelty was alluring and inflicting sufferance appeasing, also when the dolls were real. Many of his victims ended up taking their lives; some had to be get rid of, but he managed to do it so discreetly that nobody ever noticed their disappearance. Also money had never been a problem; no one beat him in gambling or in promiscuous deals; whatever gory or treacherous job was his. Too busy for regret or guilt, unaware of the existence of repentance, he went straight ahead pleasing his senses and pocket till he met Glenda, that with witchy eyes and a vampiric lure ensnared him in a bond of lust and passion. The infernal flames couldn't have burnt him more than the desire stirred by her feverish touch.

"You are most wicked and that's why I like you," she whispered one night to her lover, "such an unscrupulous soul can be nothing but appealing and desirable, darling."

Her words flattered him. He didn't know much about her, but the arcane veil hanging upon her suggested an innate mystery even more entrancing than her seductive arts.

Their delirious pleasure devoured them and they spent most of the time indoors except for a few strolls in the surrounding countryside.

The snow had hit heavily that winter, and the fields, barns and the few houses with its inhabitants whether mortals or spectres, appeared on the point of being swallowed by such ghastly whiteness. The lanes unfurled melancholic before them and the trees like multi-armed skeletons, reclined their barren tops and stretched out their branches when Glenda passed by as though greeting a well-known person.

Despite nobody was around in such a dreary setting, Leopold sensed they were not alone. Someone was lurking somewhere. He would turn round abruptly, but only void and stillness lay before him.

His lover looked diverted by his foolishness as though taking pleasure in the torment caused by such a perceivable yet invisible, impendent doom.

The graveyard was a mandatary stop. The place seemed the wind's favourite spot and especially in that season, it gave its best unsettling performance alternating eldritch shrills with consuming laments that reached the heart.

Glenda would roam among the graves before heading towards two tombs, one next to the other and remain there for a long while as if communicating with the spirits inside. Then she would smile slyly in the guise of bidding farewell and walk away without a word.

Leopold recalled a weird story about two local girls; they were so depraved that the devil wanted them to become his mistresses. He took out their hearts and burnt them to impede any form of regret and repentance. Their afterlife was spent flaming lustfully at his feet when not helping him recruiting souls.

He wondered if he had spared their bodies at least, and where the lascivious bones were interred... if ever they had existed...

Leopold would have done anything for his lover, followed her everywhere, even in the creepy property she wanted to purchase.

The structure was bleak, the rooms damp and dark, and the thick and uncouth vegetation surrounding it impeded whatever view on the outside. The secular oak that towered above such wilderness and decay seemed to house all the fowls of the area. At night time, a horrifying cacophony filled the blackness as dark wings glided around the tree.

He wasn't scared of course, but unusually disturbed.

They had just moved in when Lorna, Glenda's cousin, visited them.

With long black hair, a protruding chin and the carnation as yellow as a skinned goat, she was the perfect image of a witch.

Just like the house, he detested her at first sight.

If not a witch, she surely was some supernatural demon that had rocketed up from the infernal viscera.

There was something strange about the two girls, but while in one the oddity was enticing, in the other it was definitely disgusting.

After showing her around the house, Glenda took her into the cellar to get a bottle of wine. They remained down for quite a while and once back, they looked drunk.

They spent the whole evening gazing at each other so morbidly as if their glances mesmerised them, then Lorna took her cousin's hand and placed it on her heart and both laughed wildly at what appeared a deadly joke.

"It's still burning," giggled Glenda.

The rapture was so strong that Leopold wondered if there was something more than mere affection.

Whatever, he was sure they had conjured something… something baleful.

When Lorna left, Glenda followed her. That was the first of her many absences, and Leopold had to adjust to long periods of solitude in the fatiscent house.

Once alone, just before nightfall, wails and hisses resounded in the halls as though announcing the arrival of uncanny guests. The eerie sounds were even louder than the ones echoing from the oak tree where he swore, late one evening, he saw Lorna standing right beneath it.

169

Also the lugubrious shadows that passed by seemed real. They headed to the cellar's door that inexplicably sprang open to let them in. What was going on down there?

Sometimes, he even saw the two cousins among them, all responding to a call from the spectral abyss.

His boldness was beginning to forsake him. Horrible stories of punishment, of merciless tortures inflicted to those who had sinned crammed his mind...

For the first time, he regarded himself a sinner.

A cascade of shivers invested him, immediately followed by fits of anger and shame.

Draining a whole bottle of wine wasn't enough to wash away such stupidity.

All that damned house's fault! At the least, it was haunted. Those uncanny creatures had lived or were still living there.

Their presence was sensed in all rooms. The purple curtains continually rustling were their hiding place while waiting to populate the halls.

Whenever he entered, the fireplaces started whistling and wailing. His nefarious deeds would reel before him till the flames died... just like his victims, the ones he had taken their money, honour or life.

The most ominous part of the house though, was the cellar, a gelid cave at such a profundity that its steep staircase certainly, led to the underworld.

Glenda kept there their most precious bottles and he hated when she asked him to go and fetch one. No sooner he had entered than the door snapped shut; the adamant slam always made him shiver; to add to it, most often the light wouldn't turn on or when it did, it turned off a few seconds later and left him in complete darkness. Behind him, the sound of steps was recurrent.

He remembered when on not finding Glenda in bed one night, he searched all over the house and on approaching the cellar's door, loud cackles and giggles resounded from the keyhole. He descended and spotted his mistress in her crimson nightgown, her eyes, incandescent torches, drinking and laughing as if in company with an invisible presence. On seeing him, she turned round and sneered; then she crushed the glass with her fingers, blood mingled with the wine, and her hands turned purple.

Was she merrymaking with the devil?

Surely, the house was cursed. Haunted would have been far better.

As time passed, Glenda was away more often. Leopold grew tense, extremely irascible and kept imprecating against the nightly shadows that more and more gained consistence.

One after the other, they revealed their mortal identity; before him slid their unshrouded zombie corpses, all victims of his depravity. He realised they had been after him since his arrival.

It wasn't a trick of his imagination for the features, despite the long lapse of time, were so alike to the unfortunate souls' ones that those frightful figures couldn't be fake... simply dead and revengeful.

This time his solid armour definitely broke down and an incommensurable terror seized him.

At once and altogether, he discovered fear, horror and despair. The emotions overwhelmed him, made him cry, shout, implore and turned him into a complete wreck, just like his victims before being axed in one way or the other, by his wickedness.

Their wretched faces were an irrevocable condemn and a promise of imminent punishment.

The night was stormy, streaks of lightning flashed inside and outside the house when he saw smoke filtering from the cellar door. As if driven by a mysterious force, he rushed down and once again caught sight of Glenda now merrymaking with his victims' ghosts and Lorna.

Then a horrid figure with pointed ears and a tail appeared. The girls ran towards him and Glenda pointed her finger at Leopold.

"You've done a good job, my dear," said the diabolic presence. "Lorna assured me I could have counted on you."

Leopold stared at them horrified while the shadows were laughing coarsely and swaying as if prey of a frenzy.

The moment had arrived.

He was about to run back up when a boiling hand grasped his shoulder, "Only the devil can get away with such wickedness, man, and only he can choose which souls to take."

That said, flames appeared apparently from nowhere and the whistling of the fire mingled with the bystanders' satanic laughter.

The burning fellow's cry thundered above all as he felt his flesh turn into ashes.

Quickly, the whole house was on fire, the blazing tongues an ominous warning in the night, once again a pitch black blanket after the tempest's fury.

The Mask (Carl Hughes)

Reflected firelight flickered in demon tongues against the chamber walls and bolted up the damp stones in the way of startled lizards seeking shelter. Below, a naked man lay face-down and spreadeagled, chained to a granite slab. For him there would be no shelter, no escape. His back and buttocks reflected the firelight too, but the sweat that greased them owed nothing to heat.

Thunder had been rumbling for hours, at first only as a remote background mutter scarcely audible above the Atlantic waves pounding this rocky corner of Scotland. Now it boomed mightily, and rolled across the moor with squalls of ice-tipped rain slanted in sheets glimpsed through each eruption of lightning.

Three other people also occupied the chamber, one of them hooded in a coarse tawny habit bound at the waist with cord. This figure stooped by the fireplace in which logs blazed with peculiar intensity. Occasionally the figure would withdraw a poker, inspect its glowing tip in silence and replace it in the flames. The two others, both kilted and with manes of Celtic-red hair and beards, stood waiting on either side of the granite slab and therefore of the naked man.

'You may harm me if you will!' the prisoner yelled above the din of thunder and wind. 'You may harm me but your heathen ways will not harm His Majesty in England!'

The hooded figure looked up from the fireplace. 'Your English king will never truly rule our land!' it declared. A woman's voice, strident and passionate, echoing from the walls. Her face was concealed by the cowl. She again removed the poker. Now, apparently satisfied with the tip glowing white, she approached the slab. At the same moment she nodded to the kilted figures and they moved to part the Englishman's buttocks.

'A curse on you,' he screamed. 'I will be avenged! May it be two hundred years, five hundred or more, I will be avenged.' He strained to turn, to look at his torturer. She merely raised her eyes to a high, circular window as if exulting at her moment to come. Lightning flared again, silhouetting many irregular stones outside that loomed like furtive, curious trolls.

The hooded woman stood over her victim with the poker. 'A simple death for you would not please me,' she said. 'May your entrails burn as your heart bursts. Even above the wind and thunder, your shrieks will be heard when this flaming instrument of justice enters your bowels.'

She stooped over the prostate figure and slowly, carefully, inserted it between his parted buttocks.

And she was right.

They entered the hotel dining room long after its advertised closing time, but the proprietor had

175

agreed to serve them because of the exceptional circumstances.

'I just hope the damned fog lifts by morning so we can take off,' Elsa McLeod said. 'I'm due in Edinburgh at noon and anyway I can't get away from this godforsaken spot soon enough.'

'I'm surprised at you, Elsa,' one of her two male companions answered. 'Scots aren't supposed to badmouth their own country, are they?'

Elsa sneered. 'We aren't all haggis-eaters and crofters. Some of us like civilisation, central heating and sprung mattresses, not sacks filled with heather.'

'I can assure you I won't ask you to sleep on a heather-filled sack, madam,' the hotel proprietor put in with a wry smile. She jumped, not having noticed him follow them into the dining room. He went on, 'And though we don't have central heating, a log fire will satisfy you equally, I'm sure.'

She gazed at him without enthusiasm. Repulsive little man, she thought. Balding, flabby and club-footed so he walked with a permanent hobble. Not exactly Mr Charisma. He had told them to call him Conrad, and he appeared to staff this benighted place alone. He'd greeted them at the reception desk, signed them in, served drinks at the bar and now apparently intended to take their orders for food.

'How many chefs d'you have standing by to cook for us?' Elsa demanded.

'Only myself, madam,' Conrad answered.

'Hmm, you surprise me. Don't exactly bankrupt yourself with high staffing overheads, do you?'

He smiled. 'There's little demand for staff in winter, but during the summer months things are much busier.'

'I suppose that's when all the screwballs come out,' Elsa muttered as he withdrew, presumably to fetch menus.

She and her two companions settled at a round, white-clothed table. Both men were her junior by a few years and the trio operated on a purely professional level. Denis Proctor, the photographer, illustrated Elsa's acerbic travel articles while Roland Sadler flew them when necessary to and from remote spots such as this. Elsa had already decided to give Sadler the push and hire another pilot. Anybody who refused to fly in a bit of fog didn't deserve her continued patronage. Not that his spinelessness surprised her, what with him being English. She'd choose a Scot next time. Just as she'd choose a Scot if ever she and Denis parted company. She wouldn't normally have gone into partnership with an Englishman anyway, of course, but Denis's pictures were good. Much better than good, actually. They often represented the difference between a sale and a rejection. That bugged Elsa, too, because any fool ought to realise that her words were the really valuable commodity, not a few bloody snaps.

'I may stroll around this place with my cameras later,' Denis said. 'It has a great atmosphere. I should get some good shots.'

'Don't make them too enticing,' Elsa told him. 'This shitheap wasn't on our itinerary, remember? And I'm not sure I want to write anything about it. Even if I do, it won't be complimentary.'

She fished a packet of cigarettes from her handbag, lit up and exhaled smoke over the table. At the same time her gaze roved about the room. Oak panelling covered half the walls, with cream plasterwork above. Low beams, original brackets for oil lamps, a few stags' heads and other dead animals: the place looked typically tourist trashy. Elsa resented historic places like this being turned into holiday spots, especially for the English.

Conrad reappeared with three menus and handed them around.

'I shall prepare your rooms as you eat,' he said. 'We don't have any other visitors tonight so it's especially pleasant to welcome you. You most of all, madam.'

'Don't give me that artificial bonhomie shit,' Elsa told him. 'And what are you doing in a bloody castle like this? You can't kid me you're native, not with a BBC accent like yours.'

'Go easy, Elsa,' Roland Sadler said mildly.

She rounded on him. 'And who asked for your opinion, mate? You're just the hired hand around here and not even a good one at that.'

Conrad interrupted smoothly. 'Actually I'm from the south of England as you've no doubt guessed, but my heart is here in the Highlands. That counts for rather a lot in these nomadic days, don't you think?'

'You know, I think I'll include you in my article after all,' Elsa told him, blinking through her smoke.

'Honoured, I'm sure,' Conrad acknowledged with a little bow.

Not when I've finished, you won't be, Elsa thought with satisfaction.

They ordered a meal of locally caught salmon with organic vegetables, Highland mushrooms in whipped cream from the home farm, and a plateful of other healthy things; but Elsa insisted on French wine rather than anything plucked from local bushes and home-made.

Once Conrad had hobbled off to his kitchen she glanced around the room again and this time her gaze were arrested by a grotesque thing hanging above the fireplace.

'What in God's name is that?' she demanded, pointing.

The photographer and pilot turned to look. 'Bizarre, that's for sure,' Denis said.

They all got up for a closer inspection, Elsa wondering how she could have missed such a monstrosity earlier.

The thing proved to be a face. Or rather, the image of a face grossly distorted as if crafted by a gargoyle-maker with a particularly perverted streak. The eyes bulged, tongue protruded from a contorted mouth opened in a perpetual silent scream and

179

agony appeared to convulse every sinew. Denis reached to touch the object.

'It seems to be stone,' he said, fingers tracing the lines of frozen torment.

Elsa jumped violently at a voice from behind. 'Ah, I see you're admiring my death mask,' it said.

'God – I wish you'd stop creeping up on people,' Elsa said.

Conrad smiled apologetically. 'I do beg your pardon. I only came to assure you that your meal is in hand.'

'What's that about a death mask?' Roland Sadler asked.

'I can't tell you much about its history but the legend is that it's the death mask of some unfortunate person tortured long ago,' Conrad said.

'And you think it's trendy to hang it here in the dining room?' Elsa demanded, outraged. 'You think diners want to look at that thing while they're eating?'

'I'm told it has adorned this room for centuries and it hardly becomes me to remove it now, madam.'

His attitude and the abomination on his wall confirmed Elsa's dislike of the man and all he represented. She returned to the table, determined to put the monstrous mask out of her mind if she could. But despite her revulsion she found herself drawn morbidly towards it. Again and again her eyes strayed that way, repelled but fascinated. Over dinner she spoke far less than usual.

180

The two men adjourned to the bar afterwards while Elsa made use of a vestibule payphone to call her lover Alex in Edinburgh. In this hellhole, she couldn't get a signal for her smartphone. Alex had been expecting her back that evening, of course, and sounded surprised when she explained about the plane being grounded due to a bit of fog and a craven English pilot.

'There hasn't been a mention of fog on any of the radio weather reports,' he said. 'In fact they talk of high winds and rain.'

'Well, you can take it from me there's something thicker here than a Scotch mist and that spineless bastard Roland Sadler refuses to fly in it,' she told him. 'Which means I'm stuck in a great bloody awful castle of a place run by a slimy toad with a club foot.'

Just then Conrad hobbled by and she knew he must have overheard. The knowledge embarrassed her, but only for a moment. It wasn't as if she'd insulted him. Merely spoken the truth and if the truth hurt – well, she couldn't be blamed for that.

It was getting on for midnight when Conrad escorted the three to their rooms. They had to climb a staircase that rose into dark regions, the lintels connected by ornate posts topped by lions' heads. At the top, a Victorian grandfather clock broodingly ticked out the time. Visitors faced a long corridor lined by suits of armour, old landscapes in oils and lighting so dim that the shadows appeared to congeal in corners.

181

'I would have preferred to accommodate you in our annexe at the back but I'm afraid it couldn't be prepared at such short notice, madam,' Conrad told Elsa. He reminded her, with his rolling gait, of a crippled gnome among all these relics of long-ago things. 'However, I can offer you our best room. The gentlemen, I'm sure, won't mind somewhat smaller but very comfortable quarters.'

He showed the men to their rooms first and accompanied Elsa to hers at the far end of the corridor.

'As you see, I've made it as welcoming as possible,' he said, pushing open the door and standing aside so Elsa could enter first.

'Well, I've seen worse,' she admitted grudgingly. A log fire crackled in a triple-sized grate while a Regency four-poster bed rose majestically against one wall, its twisted columns of old mahogany supporting a canopy enveloped in Orkney lace and embroidered Hebridean cotton. The other furnishings were also antique, perhaps Queen Anne or early Georgian, all in smoked and highly polished oak and the panelled walls were decorated with oil paintings of Highland glens, hunting parties and shaggy cattle.

'Then I'll bid you goodnight,' Conrad said. 'I trust you shall sleep well and won't be disturbed by our resident ghost.' He smiled at that last word and began to back out.

Elsa stared at him. 'D'you take me for a dummy?' she asked.

He paused, eyebrows rising. 'Madam?'

'Resident ghost, my arse. You can save all that spooky guff for wide-eyed tourists.'

'You mean you doubt the existence of supernatural forces?'

'Doubt? No, mister. Doubts are for the feeble-minded. I'm telling you there's no such thing as the supernatural. End of subject. Now goodnight.'

Conrad hesitated. 'Of course you can believe or not just as you wish, madam, but I assure you that we do indeed possess a ghost – a rather famous one. Or infamous, depending on your viewpoint. It isn't of my making. Indeed, you can say I acquired it along with the rest of this property. I've never seen it myself but I understand it walks the corridors, lamenting who knows what and tapping on the walls and doors.'

'Yeah, and I suppose it plays bagpipes on the battlements too?'

'Not that I know of, madam, but as I say, I've never encountered it myself.'

Elsa exhaled noisily down her nostrils. 'Then if it shows up I'll send it along to visit you with a flea in its ear. Now if you don't mind, kindly bugger off because I'm tired.'

Conrad bowed and withdrew.

After his departure Elsa moved across to the floor-length brocade drapes covered her window. She swept them back and gazed into the Highland night. A Highland night now clear of fog and unpolluted by artificial lighting. A near-full moon had risen, gleaming on the distant pines and cedars and washing blue-white over the gables of a

183

projecting wing of the house to her right. Quietness pressed in, total but for the crackling of those logs in the grate.

Elsa shuddered. Irrationally, she disliked this place almost to the point of abhorrence. Fleetingly she even considered checking out and ordering Roland Sadler to fly her to Edinburgh now, before the fog had a chance to descend again. But she guessed he would refuse at this hour and anyway she couldn't be bothered. She really did feel weary.

After a moment she pulled the drapes back across her window, glad to shut out the night.

She awoke with a jolt, disturbed by something she couldn't identify. What time it was she didn't know but the fire had burned down to a bed of glowing embers. Then she jumped as light flared beyond the drapes of her window, briefly outlining on the brocade a score of groping tree shadows.

'Only lightning, for God's sake,' she murmured, angry at her nervous reaction. Distant thunder boomed around the mountains and hills, accompanied by a sudden dismal wind. How gothic, she thought. No doubt the ghost of McTavish or whatever its name happened to be would soon begin its tour of the place.

With a sigh she settled back into her pillows, staring at the embers and seeing in them a multitude of shapes that undulated and insinuated into each other like worms. For some reason the patterns reminded her of that grotesque mask downstairs in the dining room and she shuddered, as she had at the window.

'This dump gives me the creeps,' she told herself. Then, realising what she had said, she frowned and added, 'By creeps I don't mean fear, I mean a pain in the butt. It doesn't scare me, just brasses me off. Yeah, that's what I'm saying.'

She closed her eyes, waited for the numbness of sleep to touch her limbs again. Strange thoughts meandered through her mind, thoughts without substance: more a stratum of patterns such as those in the embers, meaningless but discomfiting. Then she jolted back to full alertness.

'What the hell is it now?' she demanded aloud.

Not thunder or lightning this time, but some stupid sod making a noise in the corridor. Pretending to be McTavish or whoever. Groaning. And tapping on doors. Audible even above the rising wind and distant crash of Atlantic waves on rock.

'If that's Denis Proctor playing silly buggers I'll castrate him,' she seethed.

More groaning, more tapping, coming closer.

'Get back to bed and let me sleep, you dickhead,' she yelled.

The Gideons had thoughtfully left a Bible on her bedside table. Elsa picked it up and flung it at the door but missed. It crashed into the wall instead and fell in a creased heap. The groans became louder. Someone tapped at her door.

Elsa was furious. She leaped from the bed and grabbed her dressing gown, too tired and irritated for games at this time of night.

By now the groans had moved on. Other doors were being tapped on along the corridor.

'What game d'you call this?' she demanded, wrenching open the door and stepping out into the passage.

To her left a dark, hooded figure prowled through the coagulated shadows, moaning softly. Of course she knew instantly that it wasn't her joker photographer Denis Proctor. The club-footed roll proved a dead giveaway.

'Is this your idea of a weird joke, Mister Fricking Conrad the cripple?' she called. 'Only, you see, you don't impress me one bit and I mean to give you and your hotel the sort of crappy write-up that'll make the plague seem inviting.'

The figure hobbled on as if it hadn't heard, still groaning.

'Look at me when I talk to you,' Elsa shouted.

It continued moving away, retreated out of sight into deeper shadow, then she heard it clumping down the staircase.

Elsa was determined not to allow the warped hotel proprietor any satisfaction at her expense. She clutched the dressing gown more closely around her and stalked after him. She'd kick away his bloody club foot and send him arse over shit downstairs, then they'd see who had the last laugh.

'Get real, you bloody idiot,' she bawled when she reached the top of the staircase. The reply, if such it could be called, consisted only of more low moaning, more tapping on woodwork. She hesitated for a second before beginning the descent.

The figure didn't appear to move quickly but even so it reached the hall well before Elsa. A mere 20-watt frost-shaded lamp glimmered down there, boosted occasionally by flares of lightning that bounced off panelling and the oil paintings of long-dead aristocrats. Elsa saw the figure hobble across more furtive shadows and slip through an open doorway and she heard its feet on a flight of stone steps presumably led to the cellar. A few seconds later Elsa reached the doorway and hesitated again before continuing her pursuit.

She shivered because the whitewashed underground walls reeked of dampness and chill that immediately enfolded her. From somewhere far below an orange-yellow light danced a weird tarantella, serving to silhouette the hobbling form ahead. Its feet scrunched on the gritty steps but all moaning and tapping had ceased since it left the hallway.

Elsa gained on the figure although not as quickly as she ought to have done, given its clumping, clumsy gait, and it reached the foot of the steps still well in advance of her. An open doorway gaped to the left, spilling out the curious dancing light that now appeared to convulse around the floor. Head bowed, the figure passed through the doorway. This time Elsa didn't hesitate. She followed.

And instantly wished she hadn't.

She found herself in a stone chamber, like a lofty cell, with walls glistening beneath centuries of green and yellow fungus. A high, round window set at what must have been the outside ground level briefly revealed sheet lightning through a festoon of cobwebs, while the raging wind and storm-driven sea sounded louder, more threatening.

Elsa saw immediately the source of the dancing shapes she'd glimpsed from the steps outside: logs were blazing with peculiar intensity in a wide fireplace, their reflected light flickering in demon tongues against the walls and bolting in the way of startled lizards seeking shelter. Elsa sensed at a primeval level that she ought not to have been lured to this place.

The hooded figure had halted by a granite slab, still with its back to her. Elsa advanced no more than two paces before swinging half around, startled by the presence of two other figures. Denis Proctor and Roland Sadler had been positioned behind deep lintels on either side of the doorway. They were watching her, unsmiling. Denis heaved the door shut, turned a massive iron key and pocketed it.

'What the hell's this all about?' Elsa demanded. Her heart lurched and she hoped the tremor in her voice couldn't be detected above the thunder.

The two men didn't reply; simply went on watching. And the hooded figure remained motionless. Its coarse habit, bound at the waist with cord, had a tawny hue like the hide of a fox. She noticed this inconsequentially. Felt more

188

apprehensive about a set of chains coiled on the stone floor, attached to the slab.

'Bollocks to this,' she said with synthetic defiance. 'You're messing around with the wrong sort of bitch here, guys. I'm not some wilting violet who'll pass out with fright at your dumb tricks.'

She strode forward, intending to snatch off the hood of her club-footed tormentor. Drag it off, wrap it around his neck and choke the repulsive little cretin with it.

The figure may have heard her coming. At any rate it wheeled to confront her.

Wilting violet she may not have been, but Elsa would have screamed at that point if her throat hadn't constricted and forced back the sound so that it almost tore her lungs. She halted, jerked a pace in retreat, reached for a support that didn't exist.

It wasn't Conrad after all. Wasn't a ghost either. Or at least, not any ghost conceived of in even her most baleful nightmares. From deep inside the cowl, a pair of living eyes glittered with a malevolence that could only have come from the open vaults of Hell. And the eyes weren't contained in a face but in the contorted hideousness of the death mask. Only now the mask had developed both life and a feral depravity, as if all its frozen suffering and grotesqueness had been wrenched back from the grave — wrenched back and endowed with a desire to wreak terror.

Even as the glittering eyes held Elsa mesmerised, she realised that Denis Proctor and Roland Sadler had moved up on either side of her.

Through a trance of terror she became aware of them ripping off her gown and flimsy nightdress. She wrenched her eyes from the living death mask and yelled and struggled but in a minute they'd torn off her bra and panties and held her writhing between them. She could feel the intensity of the distant blazing logs hot around her legs and buttocks and the dankness of the walls cold against her face.

The thing in its hood stood aside and motioned to the two men. They dragged her screaming across to the granite slab, flung her on to it face-down and held her there. She continued to struggle and scream. She saw the hooded thing move swiftly, chaining her wrists and ankles so she lay spreadeagled in heavy iron manacles.

Then it spoke and the voice both chilled and shocked her because it belonged to the hotel proprietor Conrad after all.

'Surely you realised,' it said softly, 'that a curse once cast must eventually attain its destiny? Across the centuries if necessary.'

'What are you talking about, you fricking madman?' Elsa screamed.

By way of reply the robed arm lifted and a finger pointed to the high-up window. Elsa forced back her head to look. Lightning flashed, silhouetting a line of irregular stones that loomed like furtive, curious trolls. Tombstones, of course. Then she realised that this chamber had been constructed beneath the level of a graveyard.

'My annexe is almost ready for you now,' the hooded thing said, still pointing, having to speak more loudly as the wind raged outside. 'And soon there will be two masks in the dining room. An even greater talking point for my guests.'

Elsa swung her head first to the left and then to the right, silently beseeching Denis Proctor and Roland Sadler to intervene. She saw only enmity looking back.

The hooded thing had vanished behind her but she heard it poking about in the log fire.

'What's the maniac doing?' she demanded of Denis. He didn't answer.

She turned the other way. 'Well – what's he doing?' Roland didn't answer, either. Simply smiled, moved out of her sight.

Then she felt hands on her buttocks, parting them so she thought they'd split even more than nature intended and she heard a shuffling on the stone floor as the hooded thing returned.

She felt something searingly hot close to her flesh, then the hooded thing spoke.

'May your entrails burn as your heart bursts,' it said. 'Even above the wind and thunder, your shrieks will be heard when this flaming instrument of justice enters your bowels.'

And it was right.

Meet the Authors

Rie Sheridan Rose multitasks. A lot. Her short stories appear in numerous anthologies, including Killing It Softly Vol. 1 & 2, Hides the Dark Tower, Dark Divinations and On Fire. She has authored twelve novels, six poetry chapbooks and lyrics for dozens of songs. She is also editor-in-chief for Mocha Memoirs Press and editor for the Thirteen O' Clock imprint of Horrified Press. She tweets as @RieSheridanRose.

Geoff Nelder lives in Manchester with his physicist wife, cycling rural lanes for thinking time.
Geoff is a former teacher, now an editor, writer and fiction competition judge. His novels include historical fantasy Vengeance Island; Scifi: Alien Exit; The ARIA trilogy; The vegan scifi Flying Crooked series with Suppose We released 2019 followed by Falling Up; Kepler's Son expected out late 2021 thrillers: Escaping Reality, and Hot Air. Collections: Incremental– 25 surreal tales more mental than incremental.

SJ Townend hopes that her stories take the reader on a journey to often a dark place and only sometimes back again. SJ won the Secret Attic short story contest (Spring 2020), has had fiction published with Sledgehammer Lit Mag, Hash Journal, Ghost Orchid Press, Bandit Fiction, Black

Hare Press, Black Petals Horror Magazine, Ellipsis Zine, Gravely Unusual, Gravestone Press, Holy Flea, Horla Horror and was long listed for the Women on Writing non-fiction contest in 2020. She has also written and self-published two dark mystery novels, both of which are available to purchase elsewhere: (Tabitha Fox Never Knocks, Twenty-Seven and the Unkindness of Crows). Follow her on Twitter: @SJTownend

Stephen Lang has harboured a lifetime love of all things terrifying. His short stories have appeared in the Six Six Sixth, Seventh, ATEth and Ninth Books of Horror (BHF Books), Step into the Light (Bag of Bones Press) and Sirens Call magazine. Stephen lives in Bristol with his family and an elderly black cat.

Paul Edwards is a life-long horror fan and writes his own twisted tales in any spare time that he can grab. He has seen three collections of stories published – *Now That I've Lost You* (Screaming Dreams), *Black Mirrors* (Rainfall Books) and *Night Voices* (Demain Publishing), the latter being a joint-collection with author Frank Duffy. Paul is also a fan of role-playing games, rock music and rough Somerset cider.

Olivia Arieti lives in Torre del Lago Puccini, Italy, with her family. She writes drama, poetry and fiction. Her stories have appeared in several magazines and anthologies including, *Enchanted*

Conversations, Enchanted Tales Literary Magazine, Fantasia Divinity Magazine, Forgotten Tomb Press, Horrified Press, Infective Ink, Pandemonium Press, Sirens Call Publications, Blood Song Books, Black Hare Press, Pussy Magic Magazine, Stormy Island Publishing, Breaking Rules Publishing, Scarlet Leaf Review, Iron Faerie Publishing, Dark Dossier Magazine, Paramour Ink Press, Raven and Drake Publishing.

Rickey Rivers Jr. was born and raised in Alabama. He is a Best of the Net nominated writer and cancer survivor. His work has appeared in the JJ Outre Review, Stellium Literary Magazine, Fabula Argentea (among other publications).

Tom Leaf lives in a house with an unpleasant basement, he has no pets, he practices his smile almost every day and has been scrawling words in various notebooks - both lined and unlined - for some years now. Some of his writing makes sense. Thomas is a founding member of the Alcalet Archive and knows that he should be engaging with people on social media whilst developing an effortlessly intriguing bio. He can't right now - he's too busy writing the kind of stories he would like to read.'

Liam A. Spinage is a former philosophy student, former archaeology educator and former police clerk who spends most of his spare time on the beach gazing up at the sky and across the sea while his imagination runs riot.

Thomas M. Malafarina (www.ThomasMMalafarina.com) has published seven horror novels, as well as seven collections of horror short stories. He has also published a book of often strange single panel cartoons called Yes I Smelled It Too, as well as a Microsoft based technical manual called Link-Tuit. He has written and published more than 200 short stories. All of his horror books have been published through Hellbender Books an imprint of Sunbury Press. (www.Sunburypress.com).

Sandra Stephens is a writer living in Alaska with her husband and chocolate Labrador, Jake. She has published several shorts in the horror genre, and while she doesn't always write horror, she likes to imagine the most horrific turn of events in any circumstance, making her an excellent dinner party conversationalist.

Carl Hughes is a writer and journalist who has worked for the national and provincial press in the UK and has had his articles published worldwide, from the UK to Australia, India to the US. His fiction has appeared in many anthologies and magazines and he has won numerous writing competitions. He specialises in writing about the offbeat and bizarre, with a special love of horror and *Twilight Zone*-type stories. He is married and lives in Norfolk with wife Linda.